I0537819

ALL IS WELL WITH THE TRIBE

Michael Gudeman

All Is Well With the Tribe

By
Michael Gudeman

Copyright © 2022 Michael Gudeman
LittleBearstribe@gmail.com
ISBN # 978-1-7376935-2-9
Edited by Nancy Gudeman

Introduction

The god, gods, or goddesses, if there are any, seem to have chosen not to reveal themselves in a personal interaction. The choice to believe has mostly been left up to the individual to consider whether their life is fated or a result of their own free will. Occurrences happen, forks in the road, events that can be interpreted as the finger of the divine or just dumb luck. Does one win the lottery out of pure chance, or is it gifted with intent?

Little Bear searched for signs, some kind of interaction for guidance in the purpose of his life and questioned the sights and sounds around him. Long Cloud believed and made a fatal decision about what he saw as an act foretold by the spirits in his past. Broken Horn heard the call and went off on his final journey, not knowing that either chance or the Spirits were not finished with him yet. We cannot see the wind but feel its presence and do not know if it was sent to move us or if it changes our course for no reason. We have the freedom to choose what we believe.

CONTENTS

CHAPTER 1 - TRANSITIONS

It was a late spring evening with the smell of new grass that rode upon a light breeze speaking of rebirth after a long winter. Looking at the dark forms of trees one could feel the life flowing up their trunks, out the branches, and into the new leaves. Power and strength radiated from all directions. The world was alive; its energy swaying fresh as if newly born. The gentle sounds of the approaching night let you know you were never alone; the land was alive with plants, insects, and animals large and small. Little Bear stood just outside his camp waiting for the signal to enter for his part in the ceremony, his rite into manhood.

How many had gone before him he mused. When he asked this question of his uncle Long Cloud, his answer was that all the men of the tribe had always gone through the rite of manhood, but no one knew how many generations that was. All of the men, Little Bear thought, had gone through the rite. A few died on occasion, fallen from a cliff, prey to a bear or cougar, or killed by an enemy tribe, but what was manhood if you did not prove yourself through the rite. Prove yourself, Little Bear thought. I will prove that I am the son of my father Three Suns, a great warrior, able hunter, and a good provider for the tribe.

Little Bear's mind wandered back to the day when Three Suns had gone out hunting three winters back on a cold and clear morning with a small party of braves. After several hours they spread out to cover more ground, Three Suns headed up towards

1

Lone Wolf Ridge hoping to gain a commanding view of several shallow valleys. As noon approached, thick black clouds rolled down from the northwest like the dust clouds of stampeding buffalo. They engulfed Big Horn Peak and the Spirit Mountains. A frigid wind blew before them which soon became a blizzard. Nothing could hold it back. The hunting party headed for the safety of camp; only Three Suns never returned. For three days the storm raged, then two days of constant snow, on the fifth day the weather let up enough for the strongest braves to search for Three Suns. With snowshoes made from cedar branches, a buffalo hide worn as a cape that could serve as a blanket if needed, a knife, bow and arrows, and a small bag of dried meat to keep the search going for several days, the braves broke up into five parties of four each. One party went Northwest through a light wood towards Spirit Mountain; another to search Lone Wolf Ridge. Two parties went to the valleys below Lone Wolf Ridge, and the last party searched all the ground between the foothills and camp. After three days of searching the parties started returning. They brought back whatever game they came across, but no sign of Three Suns was ever found.

Little Bear had unconsciously turned around and was looking towards Lone Wolf Ridge, "I want to be a good brave like you were," he whispered into the dark. Little Bear knew his father would never return. Death was a reality of life, the next step of a path that all would follow, that he was on the path that his fathers before him had walked. A week after the braves returned, the tribe accepted that Three Suns had died. Life was precarious at the best. Energy and focus were needed to maintain it. Hanging on to false hope was a luxury that could tip the balance of life to ruin. Knowing his father was dead was a hard truth, but there was comfort in that certainty. Those days of hoping for his father's return were filled with fear and emptiness, days that seemed like years that would never end. Then his uncle Long Cloud came into their lodge. His mother's eyes brightened for a moment, Long Cloud stood there, his form slightly swaying, looking more drained by anguish than by his long days of searching for his brother. Tears usually would not flow from his eyes, at least not on the outside as Long Cloud kept all emotion to himself, but this flow he could not keep inside.

"Three Suns has gone to his fathers." He said in a voice softer than his usual quiet tone. His strong dark eyes looked like the reflection of dark skies on still waters. "We could not find his body and he has not returned; there is no hope that he has survived. We shall all mourn his passing."

Long Cloud was concentrating on each breath he was taking, harnessing all the strength he had to keep his sorrow from overcoming him. Red Bird knew this was coming, she had been praying to the Spirits between spasms of tears. Now it was over; all hope gone. Sitting on her bed of buffalo skins, she pulled her knees up to her chest, tightly held on and let what tears she had left fall. Little Bear felt helpless but knew he had to become a man early. He had to become a man for his mother; he felt he must become a man like his father for the sake of the tribe.

"I will see to your needs." Long Cloud spoke with an odd uneasiness in his voice; he felt he had to say something, anything, and knew that he did not know what, so he just spoke without thinking.

Red Bird looked up with a confusion of emotions. Part of her wanted to scream that no one could replace Three Suns, but the contrasts were too much to take in. Before her stood Long Cloud, normally a tower of strength and calmness who rarely spoke. He was slightly fidgeting, uneasiness in his eyes that now showed tears, and hesitation in his voice. Normally when he spoke, it was with well thought out ideas in a calm and confident tone. You could count on Long Cloud; the sound of his voice would bring a sense of calmness that seemed as natural as the earth beneath one's feet. What his habitual voice and words conveyed was, "Everything is under control; wherever we go it will be alright." Long Cloud was a fixture in the tribe, like a towering tree that was planted firmly and did not move. In his shadow there was safety, a presence that all knew and trusted. No one worried when life's storms came because he was there.

These words spoken did not seem to be the words of Long Cloud. No comfort came from them and the power behind them was gone; replaced by that of a broken man, a hurting human being. Three Sun's death was going to be hard on Red Bird and the tribe, but the tribe had seen worse and Long Cloud was always there, strong and firm, leading the way. He was shaken to the core by this one death. Red Bird now realized that Long Cloud was a man, and this rock of a man could be hurt like any other. That realization startled her more that she could imagine; this seemed a different Long Cloud than the one she had always known.

There was a change in the tempo of the drums that brought Little Bear back to the present. This was the moment he had waited for with great expectation, yet a bit of fear of the unknown was mixed in with the excitement. He moved forward, approached the circle of his tribe who were surrounding the ceremonial fires and struggled not to stumble as his steps stiffened with the realization that this was the moment that he had waited so long for. The fires in the center, two separate blazes with a narrow path between them burned brightly causing Little Bear to stop momentary to let his eyes adjust. He faced the path which was only a foot's breath wide that went between the flames to the ruling council. To look anywhere else would show arrogance, fear, or disrespect for the Rite of Manhood. This would reflect upon his whole life; honor was at stake and honor it would be. The importance of each step was known by all and not taken lightly by Little Bear. He had gone over and over what was to be done and the most honorable way to perform it; now was not the time to falter. Little Bear walked forward, fast enough that he and clothes would not be singed, no pain from the flames to prod him on or change his expression; but slow enough to show no fear and give respect to the rite by not rushing up on the ruling council. As he approached the fire, he took a deep breath to keep from breathing in smoke and scalding his lungs. When Little Bear walked in the mist of the fire the younger members of the tribe gasped behind him, young teens smiled imagining it was them walking between the flames, and Red Bird was proud to see her son enter manhood.

The heat of the fire was intense, flames leaping up shoulder high, some whipped to the inside curling the hairs on Little Bear's arms and legs. There was no rule of what to wear. Some wore full buckskins to be protected from the flames, but that did not show courage and that is what Little Bear wanted to do, to show courage and live up to the measure of his father, Three Suns. Instead, he chose to wear a simple loin cloth and moccasins to show no fear of the flames. The heat of the flames stung as Little Bear walked. Had he known this was going to happen he would have darted forward diminishing the moment, but he was not going to let that happen. The pain was soon to be over. Little Bear emerged on the far side of the fire and walked deliberately step by step at an even pace up to the ruling council and stopped, his limbs glad to be cooling down with a light breeze coming from behind the council pushing the heat back towards the flames.

The ruling council was composed of six members, Long Cloud, Four Horns, Grey Eyes, Silver Fox, Chief Rolling Thunder, and the medicine man, Black Eagle. Black Eagle spoke with the Spirits, was wise with years, and could convince anyone to follow his ideas with words alone. No one questioned his wisdom. His role in the Rite of Manhood was to beseech the Spirits for a sign to know what was to be the task of each new brave. A small pouch hung around Black Eagle's neck that held the oracles of the Spirits, a mixture of scarce rocks, a feather, and small bones, all infused with magic to show the will of the Spirits. Black Eagle would chant a request over and over with the drums beating softly in the background until he was moved to empty the contents of the pouch on a buffalo skin laid before him. Then the Spirits would speak to Black Eagle through the positions of the oracles; this would tell of their will. The task was of two parts. First was a physical challenge to perform, a task to demonstrate the new brave was ready to become a man.

5

Secondly this task would reflect on the role in the tribe the new brave was to take on. The tasks usually lasted three to four days of being out on their own and would usually involve hunting a specific animal, finding a distant plant or herb, or gathering a special wood from a tree not found in the local area. The task was not as important as was being out on their own for a few days so that in being alone, the Spirits would have greater chance of speaking and of being heard. The new brave would take with him one skin for warmth, a knife, bow and quiver of arrows, and one day's ration of food.

Chief Rolling Thunder was about fifty summers old, still strong in stature and wise in rule. Many times, Rolling Thunder had led attacks on enemies in defense of the tribe, usually in response to their aggression or encroachment on the tribe's land, but always after agreement of the council. He feared no one but never let his lack of fear lead him into rash decisions, Rolling Thunder was a Chief that everyone gladly followed.

Long Cloud, like the other three members of the council, was a brave warrior over thirty summers old, not known for making rash decisions, a good hunter, and looked up to by the tribe. It gave Little Bear a bit of comfort in approaching the council seeing his uncle there among them.

Little Bear stood before the council, the nervousness fading away like the heat he had passed through. This was a festive occasion, a new brave, a sign the tribe was continuing into the future. The council wore welcoming looks upon their faces, though not to the extent of diminishing the sacredness of the rite. They were remembering their rite of manhood years ago, a memory every brave was proud of. Whether easy or hard, that was the defining moment when one became a provider and protector of the tribe, a place of honor. These council members looked upon Little Bear feeling proud of him and seeing a little of themselves in him. Long Cloud had his usual stoic look, yet a little bit of pride shown through. He had taken over the role of father after Three Suns had not returned and was now proud of Little Bear entering manhood as any father would be. Black

Eagle watched intently, sizing Little Bear up, for the tribe's sake he had to hear the Spirits correctly, and knowing each youth helped him interpret their will. Looking at how he stepped, was his head held up in false pride, was his poise of arrogance, expectation, or fear, all of these spoke to who a person was. Black Eagle knew how to read the signs of a person's heart and with the importance of the rite and for the sake of the tribe, he searched deeply to know Little Bear's very soul.

Little Bear had made the first step, shown courage before the flames, not acted rashly but controlled himself on his entrance. The council liked what it was seeing. He stood there in front of his leaders whom he knew well and of their good will towards him, but to ask to join the ranks of these mighty braves at his young age of fifteen summers seemed daunting.

"You have come through the flames to enter manhood Little Bear." Rolling Thunder said in a solemn but friendly manner. "Fifteen summers is a bit early; one more summer would be better."

Little Bear's heart dropped, his whole body was suddenly drained of energy, and a flush of embarrassment overwhelmed him as his gaze lowered to the ground. This was not how it was supposed to be; why had they let the ceremony begin if not to complete it he wondered.

Rolling Thunder continued, "but you know of your heart and soul, and if the Spirits agree, so it shall be."

Like shedding a heavy load, Little Bear felt relief. Surely the Spirits would know how badly he wanted this, how he had grown quickly, stepping into the role of his father where he could. Long Cloud took him on many hunts, taught him to fight, and survive on his own. When in camp there were many tasks to be done, yet there was always time to help his mother, and to teach the little ones of the tribe what he knew. Every task had new meaning since his father did not return. He felt the responsibility, and duty to his family. Duty to the tribe was a voice constantly heard in his head, a voice that was there just like the air he breathed.

Rolling Thunder smiled, it was obvious Little Bear was not acting out of conceit, nor being pressured from without. Little Bear felt the need, real or imagined, and was stepping up to the task; he was becoming a man. With a nod, Rolling Thunder turned to Black Eagle. No words were needed to be said. Black Eagle looked up to the stars and started to chant, the low murmur of the drums fell into his tempo and soon they sounded as one. The words could not be understood whether spoken too softly or in a different language. Little Bear did not know and soon he stopped trying to understand their meaning. The chant went on slowly, with Black Eagle swaying to the rhythm, never tiring, never changing. Little Bear noticed the council slowly swaying to the rhythm, eyes half closed as if controlled by the chant. How strong was this magic he thought as he watched it effect on the council or was it just the beat of the drums flowing through everyone that they swayed.

Suddenly the drums stopped when Black Eagle raised his voice out of step with the rhythm, "Speak" he cried. From the pouch around his neck Black Eagle lightly dropped the contents on the skin before him, drew his hands back and gazed down intently.

Captivated, Little Bear watched, first the oracles, a feather balanced on a stone, slightly moving as the breeze swirled around Black Eagle's bent form. He sat there studying the oracles, eyes intent, brow wrinkled as he concentrated, an occasional murmur when he shifted his head from this side to that. This was not normal, Black Eagle usually read the oracles rather quickly without any trouble, but now he looked perplexed, as if the signs were not as expected or their meaning unclear.

The words of Rolling Thunder echoed in Little Bears head, "… if the Spirits agree." Could this be what was troubling Black Eagle, a message he had not seen before. What other answer could there be? The Spirits had rejected him. Little Bear sighed, cast his eyes to the ground again and felt a lump form in throat. "No, no matter the answer, I will stand tall" he said to himself. With new resolve, pure mental effort, Little Bear pulled his shoulders back, stood erect and hardened his face, like Long Cloud, so no one would see the pain within. The council also seemed uneasy. Why was this taking so long? Something was different from the usual rite. Council members were looking from Black Eagle to the oracles, to Black Eagle and back again. Nobody but Black Eagle could read them; their meaning a mystery. The Spirits only opened the mind of the medicine man to read the oracles.

Suddenly Black Eagle stood up, almost as lifted by unseen hands he simply rose to his full height without any effort. All was quiet, only the crickets in the distance and the crackling of the fire made a sound, but these were not heard as all focused their attention on Black Eagle and waited for him to speak. There Black Eagle stood, a few wisps of gray hair being blown around his face; the dancing flames cast shadows from its red glow on his worn and weathered form. The appearance of ageless wisdom emanated from his countenance. Was it the Spirits upon him or his inner self they were seeing? No one knew. The only thing agreed upon was that deep wisdom was about to be spoken. Black Eagle looked into Little Bear's eyes as if measuring his soul, then without moving his gaze spoke to Little Bear loudly enough for all to hear.

"The Spirits have spoken and none may counter. We look upon the form of a boy wanting to become a man." Black Eagle paused. No one moved; every ear was on edge waiting upon the next word. "We look at the flesh and so few see what is within. Little Bear at fifteen summers feels he is ready to cross over into manhood, to take on the responsibility of being a brave in our tribe, to use his arms to provide and protect the tribe, to stand up to our enemies, to meet the heat of the summer, the cold of the winter, the darkness of night, the brightness of day, to not fear death so that the life of the tribe may continue. These things take much strength and courage, the weight of which is a burden that weighs one down until we go the way of our fathers."

Again, Black Eagle paused, these were the words of acceptance that Little Bear wanted to hear, words that caused his heart to swell with pride and filled him with expectation. Black Eagle still stared into Little Bear's eyes and the members of the council wondered at this. It was as if Black Eagle was seeing Little Bear for the first time, trying to see through his eyes into his heart.

"Little Bear still has to grow into the body of a man." Little Bear's eyes opened wider, not understanding the flow of Black Eagle's words or the change in his tone as if he changed his mind, but he had hardened himself to bear whatever came. Black Eagle could see this, the determination to stand strong when it was questionable as to the outcome.

He continued; "The Spirits do not see as we see, as we see flesh to flesh," he took his fist and struck his chest, the thud could be heard by all. "The Spirits see spirit to spirit first and then they see the flesh." Again, there was a pause to allow everyone to hear his words and understand. Little Bear no longer braced himself in expectation of rejection, though he still stood firm. All his attention was to hear what was being spoken, an inner desire for wisdom had taken over and no thought was given to anything else. Black Eagle could sense the change and started to see the Little Bear the Spirits saw. "The Spirits speak true; they speak what they see. Little Bear, though young in flesh, is a man within."

Little Bear was relieved, his journey to manhood had begun, a little differently than those who went before, but he was being called a man. Now the task, the initiation into manhood was to come that all braves faced; Little Bear was ready.

Black Eagle continued after allowing these words time to settle in, "As we all know, after the Spirits accept one as a man, a quest is given where a new brave lives up to his calling, where he faces a challenge and will learn to hear the Spirits speak. He will come back and stand as a fellow man in our tribe. Little Bear, the Spirits have spoken, a place will be set before you upon your return, Warrior, Hunter," Black Eagle paused, now staring deeply into his eyes, "and Messenger of the Spirits." These last words were spoken hard, as if Black Eagle felt challenged in his position by a young brave with no experience. A murmur could be heard running though the tribe, no one had ever heard of this before, what did it mean?

"It has been the medicine men the Spirits have chosen to speak through, me, Morning Calf before me, Night Rider before him, Red Cloud before him, there is no knowledge of any other way, but the oracles do not lie."

Little Bear was stunned. There was a comfort when everything stayed the same, even in hardships like droughts, endless rains, battles with other tribes, knowing that the tribe had faced these before showed this was a continuing cycle and that the tribe would survive. Now something boded differently, the Spirits speaking through a warrior and hunter. This did not speak of a peaceful future and that unknown evoked fear. The hardships of life were known, death always close. Animals died that we might have life through their flesh and skins. Few members of the tribe died in old age as sickness, battle, wild animals, and even childbirth brought death at times. The life of the tribe was a balance of life and death itself, all this was known and accepted, not feared. The Spirits themselves like the stars did not change, until now.

A murmur arose as the tribe sensed the difference and Black Eagle, knowing he had to act before things got out of control, raised both arms and it was quiet. He sensed the fear and in fear the life of the tribe could suffer. He had to stop it quickly before its power spread. He knew what he said and how he said it was important; he had to express this change in a positive light that would be beneficial to the tribe.

"Our tribe has continued since the Great Spirit created all. No one knows how many generations ago that was but the tribe has always survived." The intensity of the moment was great. Black Eagle was revered for his wisdom and if there was hope, he knew of it. "Lost to us is much knowledge, like so many names of our distant fathers. Who here remembers the name of their fathers'

fathers' father and his father?" He paused giving everyone a chance to think. "Do we know that Spirits have never chosen to speak to the tribe through someone other than the medicine man? I do not know, but I do trust the Spirits and if it is their will to speak to us through Little Bear, I will welcome it."

Black Eagle's words were final and with authority. Rolling Thunder and the rest of the council saw that these words settled the murmurs, calmed many fears and they were glad. Like Black Eagle, the council had sensed the uneasiness of the tribe and knew this disquiet had to be quelled; like a herd of buffalo, uneasiness could lead to a stampede; it would be easier to soothe things now than when events got out of control.

Rolling Thunder spoke, "As Chief, I say Black Eagle speaks wisely, let us not make the Spirits angry by rejection of their decisions."

At this point fear was shifted from the unknown to the possible anger of the Spirits. People squirmed lowering their heads as if to hide their faces from man and spirit, a good sign thought Black Eagle as he scanned the tribe.

It was quiet once more when Long Cloud spoke up, "What else do the Spirits say, what is the quest?" All eyes fell on Long Cloud, so rare to hear his voice; stunned by its power and resonance that carried throughout the camp by a brave that all respected.

Black Eagle smiled within, the tribe had gone from celebration of Little Bear's rite of manhood, fear of the unknown, fear of offending the Spirits, to be brought back to the expectancy of the continuation of the rite by the strong calming words of Long Cloud. Heads turned quickly back to Black Eagle.

"This is a time of celebration; the Spirits have welcomed another brave into our tribe."

The mood was relaxing, the tribe had heard these familiar words before, and it was the natural rhythm of life. Black Eagle knew he had to prevent any more upsets from happening, but it was not going to be easy. The task in the oracles would reignite the fears of the tribe, but by not answering Black Eagle would also set the fire of fear running through its heart. As with any good leader, knowledge of using the right voice could make all the difference from panic to fears forgotten.

"Little Bear," Black Eagle called out in a loud voice that sounded like someone being welcomed after a long absence, "your quest will be one of honor that brings back wisdom to our tribe."

Little Bear noticed Black Eagle's eyes were no longer piercing into his eyes even though he faced him a mere arm's length away. Black Eagle was carefully looking into the crowd around the fire. Little Bear knew Black Eagle was also speaking loudly for the crowd to hear. He now understood the focus of Black Eagle was no longer in speaking to him but the tribe, something was going on that he was missing and he was now aware that there were two different messages being spoken.

Suddenly Little Bear remembered the time of talking to his friends when his little brother was with them. White Fawn, a young girl that all the young teens were interested in walked by. Little Bear remarked to the boys with a smile how he wished he had a fawn like this one for his own, not knowing that his mother was within ear shot. Little Bear's brother looked around for a fawn but could not see one, and asked where the fawn was. The boys laughed thinking themselves clever and said he had just missed seeing her. Red Bird frowned and sought out Long Cloud. Whenever the boys needed instruction Long Cloud was called upon. He would approach the boys and inform them that on the next day they would be going out with him on some tasks: scouting, hunting, gathering wood for arrows, a job that would entail long discussions on proper behavior and why it was important. These times of instruction were welcomed as it was an honor to go out with Long Cloud and the talks were filled with stories of the tribe and the surrounding world.

This was a wisdom he had known of, speaking with two meaning for separate people at the same time, and was now seeing Black Eagle use it. Little Bear liked its taste and waited for more. Black Eagle's voice now had a tone of excitement and longing to it as if he wished to be in Little Bear's place.

"Tomorrow you will set out on a vision quest where the Spirits will give you wisdom and guide you in the ways you are to follow. You will return a man to stand firmly with the braves of our tribe. Let us celebrate!" His words were short and with purpose, to keep the tribe on a path of normal expectations and not down into a hole of fear of the unknown. Enough words had been spoken, now was the time to move the tribe to the joy of their continuance.

With that the drums began to beat at a fast pace, the older boys jumped up in joy at seeing their friend Little Bear moving on to manhood and began to dance. Memories of his fears faded away as the tribe rejoiced.

CHAPTER 2 - THE QUEST

Black Eagle now turned his eyes to Little Bear who was still standing before him. There was much to tell him. His task being to begin at first light, a specific path to be followed unlike most other tasks, Little Bear must be ready. Time was not something to be wasted but another important matter was at hand, the tribe needed the usual pattern of events to remain as they always had. They expected to see each of the council embrace Little Bear, give him a little advice, and then for Little Bear to join them in the dancing with his friends. Calm would not remain if this pattern was broken, especially after this night's revelations. Little Bear must not be delayed. With a relaxed voice of goodwill, but eyes that commanded obedience, Black Eagle spoke: "Be ready in the morning, all will be explained before you leave at first light."

Little Bear wanted to know more, he had many questions about this night: the message of the Spirits, the meaning of Black Eagle's words to the crowd, the quest, but Black Eagle's eyes were firm and accepted no challenge. Turning to Chief Rolling Thunder, Little Bear had hoped to get a little more information but was quickly disappointed. Rolling Thunder grasped his arms firmly while saying how proud he was to welcome a new brave into the tribe, then turned to speak with Black Eagle. One by one, Little Bear got the same welcome from the other council members until lastly Long Cloud greeted him.

"Things have progressed in a way we did not foresee; go join your friends for a while and we will talk in the morning before you leave." Without waiting for a response, Long Cloud turned and went to join the council. This is the Long Cloud I know thought Little Bear as he watched him catch up with the council as they walked towards Black Eagle's tepee. As they went out of sight Little Bear noticed how calm he was, the calmness of the council seemed to have spread to him in an unseen manner and he wondered at this power of their presence.

Suddenly he was grabbed from behind by his friend Chicken Hawk. "Come on and join us in the dance, this is your celebration too." All was right in the world again, like the day dawning, everything felt right.

Black Eagle, Rolling Thunder, and the rest of the council retreated into Black Eagle's tepee. A ring of skins was set out evenly spaced around a small fire that was set more for light than warmth. Black Eagle walked in and sat opposite the entrance. Long Cloud and Rolling Thunder sat on either side of him. The air was thick not so much by smoke but by the tension of this night's ceremony. There was more to be told and the council respectfully waited for Black Eagle to speak as he sat gazing into the fire. Shadows from the fire found every crevasse on Black Eagles' face accented by the red light that landed on the well weathered flesh of this old medicine man. Black Eagle was sixty-seven summers old but tonight he looked eternal, like the rocky heights of Spirit Mountain, as old as the rocks themselves. Responsibility weighed heavily upon his shoulders and this rock of a man held it as only a medicine man could.

Black Elk took a small pouch of tobacco and packed the pipe that he had laid up earlier at his seat knowing the council would have the events of the evening to discuss. With a burning faggot from the fire held over the bowl of his pipe, he watched as little by little the flame was being drawn to the tobacco as he sucked gently, breathing in the smoke. Once lit, it was handed down the line of the council as each paused in their thoughts long enough to enjoy a few puffs. After the pipe made its first round it was time to speak. Looking into the fire, Black Eagle took a deep

16

breath, let it slowly out, and then started: "The Spirits speak and we have always listened. They direct us and we follow; they have deep wisdom and we learn from them." All heads nodded in agreement.

"Tonight, they speak again. They speak of Little Bear and of his place in the tribe, and their words are always true. I am troubled at what was said, what path is set for Little Bear to follow. Before a storm, the morning sky is red; before a flood, heavy rains fall; before trouble comes to the tribe, a mighty warrior is raised up." Black Eagle paused, drums and chanting could be heard in the distance as the tribe enjoyed the warm spring evening, sharing in the joy of Little Bear and his newfound position as full member of the tribe. In stark contrast was the mood in Black Eagle's tepee. Deep shadows and dark expectations enveloped; the council sensed trouble as the tribe was celebrating its growth. The fire crackled quietly, Black Eagle looked up and watched the wisps of smoke slowly rising to the stars, leaving through the hole in the top of the tepee. Was his mind being drawn to the fire and smoke a sign, was the tribe to go through trials of fire and the souls of its members to float up and join their fathers? Black Eagle mused for a moment, and then continued.

"The Spirits spoke of a warrior and a medicine man, a fighter and a spiritual leader, someone with authority to lead the tribe in times of battle. We have a hard time coming before us, I know not when, but it is coming"

Again, Black Eagle paused giving the council time to weigh his words. His dark eyes peered at each of those sitting around the fire waiting until everyone understood the weight of his words. His gaze stayed a long while on Long Cloud, Little Bear's uncle, now surrogate father, yet here he sat with his usual unmovable face. His deep eyes spoke of a mind constantly thinking, taking in all and considering everything. Black Eagle could not read what Long Cloud's thoughts were as he could the other council members and in this time of pending peril, he needed all the wisdom at hand to lead the tribe. Measuring his words and voice to not sound like one without answers and thereby raise alarm but in speaking in such a manner as to show his respect to the council by valuing their thoughts and ideas, he proceeded,

"What say you Long Cloud, you are closest to Little Bear, what do you see?"

Long Cloud had continued to meet Black Eagle's gaze in a way that showed he was taking in all that was being said. He had spoken before to his fellow council members on previous times, but always on matters that he knew: hunting, the nature of plants, animals, and their trends, or other tribes, their strength and weaknesses, on gauging men and what to expect from them. Now an open question was posed and it took a moment to bring the night's events into focus and combine that with what he knew about Little Bear. Long Cloud looked at the fire and decided to talk and let the answer come out as he was thinking and not wait until he was clear on his thoughts. "To read omens in the oracles have not been given to me, but the Spirits do speak to me with the words that only I hear. They show me wisdom in the lives of plant and animal, and I listen. I have taught Little Bear to hunt and track, read the signs on the earth and in the air, as a warrior to fight not only with knife and bow but by reading his enemy like a bear, lion, or wolf. I have taught him to be patient like the cat, watchful like the deer, protective like the she bear but not rash like the badger. In all things, to see, not just with the eyes but the mind; to always look for signs from the Spirits and listen to them."

"I have tried to teach him wisdom, but he is young and has much to learn. Could Little Bear grow to be a good warrior and a medicine man, I know not, but this will tell us a lot as to who he will become. I can say no more."

Black Eagle gave a gentle smile; Long Cloud spoke like a father proud of his son yet like a council member gauging a new brave. "You speak well Long Cloud, Black Eagle said in a voice that showed approval and confidence in Long Cloud's view. "As always you have said much in your few words and you speak

18

correctly. We have two things to attend to. The tribe must be prepared for whatever is to come and we must know of Little Bear's soul and train him up so he will be ready when the time of his calling comes."

The council all nodded in agreement while Rolling Thunder poised himself not as a follower but as Chief getting ready to lead the council and the tribe. Black Eagle had much sway but Rolling Thunder allowed no one else rule. He had just finished taking a few puffs on the pipe and handed it to Black Eagle with a nod signaling that he was ready to speak. "You give good council Black Eagle; the Spirits were wise in choosing you to speak their wisdom." His voice had an air of command, yet softness as one talking to a good friend. All nodded again in agreement, Black Eagle felt a warmness inside his soul at the praise coming from Rolling Thunder. As an old man of sixty-seven summers, it felt good to still be considered useful, a value to the tribe. "We will plan our preparations for the tribe after Little Bear completes his quest. Long Cloud, you are the best one here to track Little Bear, see how he fares without him or anyone else knowing you are there. We must know how Little Bear meets this challenge so we may guide him while we can."

Looking back upon Black Eagle, with a slight bow of his head to offer honor, Rolling Thunder asked, "What do the Spirits say of Little Bear's quest, how shall he be tested?"

Black Eagle looked at the fire and watched the low flames dance for a moment, clearing his mind of all else, he had to open his thoughts to the right interpretation. Slowly, closing his eyes, sitting erect, tilting his head back and looking with his mind's eye upon the oracles as they had lain, he spoke. "A strong sign was given, strength must be shown, a spiritual connection was foretold, and spiritual guidance must be found." He paused to let this interpretation take hold in his mind. "Spirit Mountain is three days journey for a strong brave; thence he shall go. Half a day's climb up the mountain there is a small lake. It is there, Little Bear will hear from the Spirits and receive wisdom." Black Eagle, sitting erect with his head still tilted back paused again to let the words sink in before continuing. He could hear the council murmuring amongst themselves, the quest was quite a bit more involved than the ones they had heard of before.

Four Horns could not restrain his thoughts and spoke aloud in the shock of the moment breaking Blacks Eagle's concentration and causing him to bring his head forward to look at him. "That would be at least seven days. Most quests are two or three days, and Spirit Mountain is in Yarric territory. Little Bear has just begun the rite into manhood but he is still a boy, how can this be?"

Four Horns' expression was of disbelief and not a challenge. His voice, a combination of surprise and concern was easy to see. Black Eagle looked at Four Horns at first with a stern glare, but quickly realized this was not a challenge of his authority. The shock of the quest not being in line with what was usual and a protective spirit for a boy who had lost his father was the cause of this outburst.

"Rest easy Four Horns," Black Eagle said in a voice of compassion as to a close friend, "I feel your concern, so let me explain." Shifting himself to face Four Horns, he took a more relaxed position knowing the importance of his every move, his every word, from the sound of his voice to the look in his eye. The council had to show that everything was in their control or the daily life of the tribe would be disturbed, distracted from their duties that kept life going smoothly. This could bring hardship to the life of the tribe. Now, Black Eagle thought, I must calm the council or all control will be lost in a lack of confidence. Four Horns has voiced his thoughts and surely others agree with him, now is the time to lead.

"I see your concern," he spoke in a reassuring manner, making sure not to chide Four Horns for his sudden words and interruption. "I also share in your feelings for Little Bear and wish not to overwhelm him in his quest, but the Spirits know what is needed and he shall not fail. Little Bear is being raised up to meet some challenge in our future; he needs to be ready to face whatever is to come. In this trial he will need to be strong, wise, and ready to act. Seven or more days seems long and hard, if he can survive two, then he will succeed in many, and with this success he will quickly gain the confidence in himself that he will need in the future. Also, unknown to Little Bear, Long Cloud will be near to take whatever action is needed to protect him from the Yarric; no better brave is there to bear this charge."

Black Eagle paused for a moment to let the council consider his words. Looking from face to face he could sense the council relaxing, accepting his words. "We must trust in the ways of the Spirits. It is they that are going to train up Little Bear in wisdom, to help him become a man. If the Spirits have chosen a place to reveal themselves to Little Bear, who are we to disagree?"

Four Horns lowered his eyes into the glowing embers and softly spoke:

"I am sorry to have spoken rashly. Your words are wise indeed."

Black Eagle had accomplished what he wanted, with Four Horns accepting his words and the rest of the council showing signs of agreement. The will of the Spirits as shown through the oracles would be done. Now was the time to strengthen the council in unity.

"You did right to speak your concerns Four Horns, for we must act together in one mind," Black Eagle said in the tone of a father to a repentant son. "The tribe will look to us as they question the oracles, we must calm them with soft words and show them that we trust in the Spirits and their directions. The quest should not be made fully known until Little Bear returns so that the tribe does not worry, only let it be said that Little Bear will be gone a few more days than usual, and no word of where. Let us be seen not as if worried but pleased as Little Bear's quest continues, that ever hour he is gone it is another hour of a gift from the spirits to us and to Little Bear."

"Long Cloud," Black Eagle said after another brief pause.

Long Cloud lifted his gaze from the ember to meet Black Eagle as he turned towards him, his stoic expression was still of one listening, considering deeply everything that was being said. "In the morning before first light, prepare Little Bear; make sure he has what he needs for this journey, plus two days ration and tell him of the path he must follow. As the stars start to fade, I will come and give him further instructions before he goes. It is then that you should go ahead as you think best to keep a watch on him. Let no one see you leave. You are to watch over Little Bear without his knowing it. He must face this alone but we need to know what occurs and how he handles this challenge if we are to help him grow. Protect him if he needs it, but secretly at all costs."

Long Cloud waited to be sure there was nothing else, no other questions, and then in his stoic way said: "It shall be so." And the pipe now came to him and he took it with a gentle reverence in both hands, puffed slowly, treating it as if it were a gift from the spirits, then passed it carefully on. Were the tobacco and the responsibility to safeguard Little Bear both a gift from the spirits? Long Cloud wondered as he turned his gaze back to Black Eagle and his stoic form returned.

Black Eagle and Rolling Thunder both wondered at Long Cloud and his calmness, his self-control. He was about to follow his nephew into Yarric territory, spy on him from a distance while at the same time, protecting him; and he had agreed with no more show of concern than if he were asked to put another log on the fire. They knew no better brave could be found to do this job. Long Cloud would be aware of all the risks and challenges. He would face them without hesitation, without fear, he was in total control of himself. What they could not see was a heart that reached to Little Bear, his brother's son. They could not see the relief he had knowing that he would be there to protect Little Bear. Nor could they see his concern for the tribe and his belief that the Spirits had spoken truly. There would be a need and Little Bear must be prepared to meet it. Long Cloud felt deeply about many things, but he would not let it show on the outside.

Rolling Thunder, seeing that all was said that needed to be said, rose to his feet and looking around at the council gave them one last word. "We must be seen this night showing no concern. Let us join the celebration and be seen giving Little Bear good-hearted advice, speaking of the joy we feel in his becoming a new brave in our tribe."

As the council was leaving, Rolling Thunder held Long Cloud back. "Make the preparations needed for yourself and Little Bear; we will speak again when you return."

Long Cloud slowly nodded his head in respect and acknowledged his instruction, and then exited the tepee. Standing there alone, Rolling Thunder spoke softly to the empty space: "My friend Long Cloud, I can trust you with whatever task you are given; you will not let me down. You shall succeed and come back. I have great trust in you, but why don't you speak more and let me know you once again as when we were young. Why have you changed so? Good luck my friend." And then Rolling Thunder left his tepee to perform the role of Chief and dismiss any fears of the tribe.

CHAPTER 3 - PREPARATION

Long Cloud walked out of Black Eagle's tepee and headed back to the center of camp in search of Red Bird among those celebrating. As he approached, people who glanced up, saw his familiar form and felt secure knowing that Long Cloud was there. It seemed odd that such a stern face would be so welcomed, but all knew that this stoic Long Cloud was there for them, like a mountain, he would never budge from being their protector. If Long Cloud was there, all was well. Seeing Red Bird up ahead talking with a group of her friends, he walked up to within a few steps and waited to be acknowledged. He did not have to wait long before the talking stopped as welcoming smiles appeared and Red Birds' friends parted to allow her to approach Long Cloud. It was a proud mother with a big smile that walked up to Long Cloud, bowed her head slightly and looked up into his eyes like a young girl, then suddenly leaned forward and wrapped her arms around him. His heart melted at her touch and Red Bird could hear its beat speed up as if calling her name. Red Bird's friends saw his face respond as if to a lover and their giggles broke the spell holding him. Red Bird was very grateful for all Long Cloud had done since Three Suns hadn't returned, from helping take care of her children to supplying their needs. She had tried to find ways to repay Long Cloud's kindness over the years, and with all this attention focused on him, her gratitude, and proximity to him, she had grown to love him.

Long Cloud looked down on Red Bird and could not help but to be moved by her eyes looking dreamily into his, that gentle smile, the closeness to her, his heart yearned for her but he still held back. With a voice of softness that caused the other women to meekly smile, Long Cloud spoke.

"Little Bear must leave on his quest at dawn; prepare for him two days' worth of food to carry with him. It is best to be dried meat so he can travel quickly. A small buffalo skin is all he will need for the nights, a knife and his bow. Black Eagle will come just before daybreak to see what Little Bear is carrying and see him off so be sure there are only two days' supply of food. He can catch or gather more if there is a need."

With this warning Long Cloud tried to look stern so Red Bird would take him seriously, but he could not put on a false face or look glaringly upon her so that his expression ended up being comical and caused Red Bird to giggle. This annoyed Long Cloud, not being taken seriously, so he quickly continued, "I will come in the morning to instruct Little Bear before Black Eagle arrives; ensure he is ready."

Red Bird quickly spoke before Long Cloud could turn and leave. "How long will he be? What is his quest?" Looking into Red Bird's eyes he could see a proud mother who trusted her son, trusted that Long Cloud, being a council member, would not let Little Bear's quest be dangerous, but she still worried as this was the first time he would be out on his own. He could not tell her the council's words nor did he want to start her worrying about the length of the trial; he could not lie and he could not reveal the whole truth. To be in battle with knife and bow was easier than this he thought.

"Little Bear will go out where he can be alone; he will wait and listen for the Spirits to come and speak to him, to teach him wisdom. The Spirits do not always act quickly but they come in their own time and there is much wisdom for him to learn. We know not how long, only that the Spirits have called him. Be pleased as the longer he is listening to the Spirits, the greater he will become. I must go now."

Long Cloud quickly turned and left feeling he had faced one of the greatest challenges of his life. He knew Red Bird would worry as the days dragged on, the memories of Three Suns not returning would come to mind, and he could not reassure her by sharing that Little Bear would be under his watchful eye. He did not look forward to the questions she would ask about his movements during Little Bear's quest, knowing that he could not answer, and those questions surely would come.

While everyone was distracted, Long Cloud walked back to his tepee, gathered a bag of provisions, his bow and quiver, and quietly slipped out of camp heading north. He wanted to be ready to follow Little Bear in the morning without anyone noticing him leave. If seen, it would look innocent enough if he was not carrying anything that looked like he was going on the quest with Little Bear or bringing extra provisions to him. As it was, Long Cloud would have to go south at first and then circle around to pick up Little Bear's trail with every effort to be made to keep from being seen. It did not seem right to be deceiving those of his tribe as among other traits, Long Cloud was known for honesty. To be acting in such a way as to give a wrong impression of the truth was a lie and that was painful for him to endure. The dark night mirrored the darkness he felt in his soul.

After going far enough not to be found, he went just off the path to where a large oak stood stretching out its dark branches into the night. This was an ideal place to store his supplies until the next day as its largeness made it easy to find and anything placed in its limbs would be lost in the tangle of branches, twigs, and new leaves that were budding out. Hopefully no animal would get into the food he was stashing, time spent gathering new stores to replace those stolen would be time not watching over Little Bear. With this task complete, he now started walking back along the trail and listening for any sign of life so not to be seen, it was not long before Long Cloud heard movement just ahead in a small clearing. Cautiously moving forward, he could make out someone hiding something in a small group of rocks. He watched as the same figure rearranged

26

the rocks, then stepped back inspecting their work, then turn back to the path and walk quickly towards camp. Long Cloud recognized the figure as Red Bird.

It was obvious what was going on as others had done the same in past rites. Red Bird was hiding extra food for Little Bear to take with him after Black Eagle saw that he only had two days ration. Long Cloud was disappointed in Red Bird but accepted that she was neither the first nor the last mother to want to help her son. Why couldn't they see that the quest was important? Each part had meaning and was meant to help their sons to grow. "Well," he thought, "this will be the first test for Little Bear." Long Cloud walked back to camp making sure he stayed close enough to keep an eye on but not overtake or be seen by Red Bird. As he walked, his eyes constantly seeing Red Bird slightly ahead, he felt his heart yearn, pleading with him to run forward and take her in his arms, to profess the love he felt for her, and to ask her to be his wife.

It was still dark when Long Cloud awoke and came to give one last talk to Little Bear before his journey. He found him sitting outside his tepee, leaning back looking at the stars with a small bundle, a rolled-up buffalo pelt, and bow and quiver beside him, a knife strapped to his thigh. Long Cloud looked down on him, then quickly sat beside Little Bear and gazed up to the stars. "Our fathers are up there looking down upon us" Long Cloud said in a matter-of-fact way. "When I was little, I would call out to them and wait for an answer."

Little Bear turned towards Long Cloud, surprised to hear him open up about himself. It felt good, like Long Cloud trusted him, welcoming him into a new level of relationship. Was this a part of being a man he wondered, to share old moments of your past?

"Did they ever answer you?" Little Bear asked with a chuckle.

"Only when I learned to listen, to hear without my ears, then they spoke and I heard as I hear them now."

Little Bear was stunned by these words and perplexed. Long Cloud was speaking as if describing the wind blowing or sun shining, as if the Spirits speaking was of no special occasion. "I

27

do not understand. You hear the Spirits speak? Why have I not heard their voices too?"

Without removing his gaze from the stars, Long Cloud answered. "I was fifteen summers when I went through the Rite of Manhood. That day I was so confident of myself and was going to complete the rite in a short amount of time and prove that I was a man. Black Eagle was younger then and came to tell me of my quest on a morning such as this."

There was a pause. Long Cloud still looking to the stars, was seeing only the memories, feeling once again the cool air of that morning as it approached on that distant day long ago. "Black Eagle spoke of an old mountain goat with one broken horn that lived in the mountains to the west. The Spirits said I was to hunt him down and bring his horns back. Many hunts I had gone on and this seemed no different except there was just one specific animal to find. How easy this was going to be I thought, to hunt an old goat. I was a good hunter back then.I was young and agile and the old goat was probably slow. What an easy challenge I thought. With my chest sticking out, arrogance in my step, and a smirk on my face I started out. A little more than a day's travel away and then for the next three days I searched the mountains tops and though there were many goats, never did I see the one with a broken horn. The third evening I shot a marmot, skinned and dressed it, then roasted it over a fire. The cool mountain air soon turned cold, the deer skin I brought offered little comfort, so sure was I that the goat would fall to my arrow the first day that I had rejected the heavier buffalo pelt that was wisely offered. Those cold nights are still frozen in my memories. Questions of whether the goat had died earlier filled my mind. Were the Spirits laughing at me on a pointless quest? Sitting close to the fire to gather most of the warmth it had to offer, I slowly chewed on a greasy piece of marmot, letting my anger grow. The stars came out, each one shining like fresh drops of water from melting snow.The sight made me feel colder and the anger grew like the darkness around me. Thousands of them shone and I thought of them as the Spirits of our forefathers looking down, seeing how an old goat was making a fool out of me. I went from anger to shame to tears. Who would call me a man now?"

Long Cloud paused again; the stars were starting to fade as the morning light was approaching. Camp noises could now be heard, rustling here and there, a child crying. Red Bird had prepared the morning meal within and came out seemingly more excited than Little Bear. "Eat your fill," she said while placing an exceedingly large portion before him.

Little Bear was eager for the story to continue but dared not speak. He did not have to wait long as Long Cloud could sense his impatience.

"I broke." Long Cloud continued after taking a bite of the food that Red Bird has set before him. "I was a proud youth being bested by an old goat. Like a young bird ready for the sky on its first venture from the nest and falling to the ground in a small heap, I huddled there hurting. It hurt more than any arrow that has pierced me since; this was my first lesson, and I had more to come." Little Bear remembered seeing Long Cloud on hot summers days, his bare chest bore many scars from many battles, how could his disappointment hurt more that those wounds he wondered?

"Being alone, in pain, not knowing what to do, I cried out, "Help me Spirits". Tears rolled from my eyes and I could taste the salt of them. "I don't know what to do". The words stung my heart. I was supposed to be a man, yet I was a crying boy who was lost in the wilderness. "Please guide me". I was no longer that proud youth. "I will follow where you lead, and I was soon to learn what it was to be a man."

"Suddenly there was a gust of wind," Long Cloud said with a start that made Little Bear flinch, "and then silent calm. The fire crackled, but all else was quiet, nothing stirred as I strained my ears to hear with expectation of the unexpected. After a few moments of no further sound or movement, I relaxed and closed my eyes, still listening to the strange calm with no thought in my mind, when I heard a soft voice. Whether this

29

was my own mind or the Spirits I could not tell, but faintly the words sounded like, "Follow, not for yourself, follow. Fear not, your task is true. Fear not. We send you". Then the crickets chirped, the fire sizzled, as grease dripped from the remains of the marmot that was suspended over the flames, and a light breeze seemed to gently blow again."

"While sitting there wondering if this was indeed the Spirits speaking or the imagination of my own mind, the moon came over the far hills lighting up the mountain side. There about two bow shots away, upon an outcropping of rock could be seen the outline of a mountain goat against the star filled sky, and I seemed to perceive a difference on one side of its head compared to the other. Real or vision I could not tell for soon it moved away and only the bare rocks and stars behind could be seen."

"That was a long cold night with little sleep waiting for the morning light so I could begin searching the rocky crag for a sign that my vision was real. Too dangerous at night to search by torch, I was losing the rashness of my youth and was starting to think before I acted. What little sleep I could get would be needed to give me a keen eye and steady hand for my bow. If this was the goat in the flesh, now having a track to follow would be easy, or so I thought back then."

Long Cloud gave a little chuckle, laughing at himself, then looked around at the fading stars. "I better hurry, Rolling Thunder will be here soon. The next morning, I rolled up my deer skin, storing it to be gathered later along with the remains of the roasted marmot. It was now time to hunt. I hurried to where the vision of the goat stood and sure enough, there were tracks. Carefully studying the tracks, I noted the size and could tell how much of a hurry he was in. The chase was now beginning, and I returned to my overconfident self, thinking this goat was soon to feel the sting of my arrow.

"Knowing how mountain goats would seek high ground, leaping from rock to rock, I determined which direction he was headed, saw the most likely ground the goat would head for and bounded off in search of more tracks. Reaching what

I considered a place that his trail would cross, I searched the ground closely, looking in places where there were sure to be at least one hoof print, but none were found. Maybe the goat was being cautious at night and was taking an easy and safe path in the dark. No goat could outsmart me, this I knew for sure. Returning to the first tracks, I slowly followed each step he took intending to hunt with focus on the trail. Soon my eagerness pushed me quicker and jumping ahead and lost the trail. I was constantly having to backtrack to the last seen hoof print and never catching up to my quarry."

"By the time the sun was hanging low in the distance, knowing I had to get back to my camp before the cold of night overtook me in its darkness, I stood erect and looked around to mentally mark this spot to continue the next day. To my surprise, camp was just a short distance off. The goat had walked in circles, never far from me, always unseen and always unheard. With the night approaching and the danger of a misstep being a fall over a cliff, I headed back the short distance, gathering wood along the way with a heart even heavier than the burden in my arms. Upon dropping my load next to the small fire pit of the night before, my heart dropped even further. There where I had slept the night before were the fresh tracks that I had been following all that day. My head hung low. I was bested by a goat, goaded by a dumb animal that circled back to walk through my camp. I was so sure I would slay him that very day. Anger flared within. I could see nothing but a vision of an old goat with a busted horn laughing at me. I was so mad that all caution left me and I screamed in rage which caused all other sounds to stop; not an animal, bird, nor insect made a sound after this outburst. With that blast of energy, the anger turned to despair. I slumped down into the silence of the night. I felt beaten. Slowly the night sounds of insects and a few birds returned as the cold swept in and the sun dropped behind distant hills. Darkness filled the sky and seeped into my soul. Quietly rousing from utter despair, I kindled a small fire, wrapped the deer skin around my shoulders and stared into the flames. I felt so little on that high mountainside. An endless sky filled with stars above looked down on me and my little fire, a little boy who brazenly bragged of being a brave, but could not find his prey, and when shown his quarry could not track an old goat. Despair turned to self-pity."

"After eating a little marmot and arranging the firewood where it was easy to reach, I drifted off into a fitful sleep. Dreams came, all of them dealing with the previous day's hunt. All ended the same way, seeing myself as a child sitting alone by a fire, not having seen my prey. I woke up cold, only embers left from the little fire that I had been tending. The moon was high but revealed nothing upon the rocks where the goat stood the night before. Adding small branches to the coals and fanning them into flames made the night a little less lonely as it drove some of the darkness back from my camp. The warmth of the fire eased some of the stiffness brought on by the cold night air; it would be a long hard night without the comfort it would offer. I looked around at the rocks, low bushes, and few trees silhouetted by the moonlight, this was a cold lonely place to be, yet this was where I must be to find this one goat and become a man. Putting a few bigger branches into the fire, I thought of the goat. He was out there without a fire or blanket to help fend off the cold. Little food grew up here; he must feel hunger at times too. He knew I was here, probably knew I was after him and wanted to kill him. Did he know fear, I wondered."

"I drifted back into a light sleep and dreamt only of the goat. First, I saw him as a young kid, leaping and jumping with other young kids; butting heads, slipping off rocks, but always getting back up. Soon he was a young buck challenging other bucks, running with strength, climbing steep cliffs, growing wiser with age. I saw him fight with an older buck, knocked over a small cliff and breaking one horn. This was the buck of my quest. The dream continued as he grew old and would fight no more. Less sure of his balance, he rarely climbed the steep rocks. The chill of the night and the cold winter days caused his old wounds to hurt and muscles to stiffen up. I saw the look in his eyes, one of pain, a longing for the season of life to end. He was standing on the eastern side of two trees that offered some shelter from the wind and was awaiting the coming of the morning sun to give him some warmth."

"When I woke up, the fire was low, and frost covered the ground and glistened in the fading moonlight as dawn was approaching. After building up the fire again, I rubbed my sore muscles from sleeping on the hard rocky ground; the cold took a while to be chased away by my little fire, the only source of comfort on this lonely mountain. I thought of my dream, of the old buck. This morning would be tough on him, frost on his hide, waiting for the comfort of the sun. I pitied him. His strength was his undoing; being strong he survived into old age, and old age was an enemy that was slowly, painfully, ending his life. I wondered if that was what would happen to me, getting to a point where it hurt just to live."

"Warming myself, eating the last of the marmot, a decision had to be made: start tracking again or hunt up some food in preparation of several more days upon the mountain. Looking back on the last few days, it was plain to see I was not the man I had hoped to be. I was not the hunter, nor the tracker, and counting on my abilities had been a failure. With a sigh I looked to the morning sky, the sun would soon rise bringing its full light. Already the vastness of the country could be seen. Finding this wise buck in it now felt daunting. "Spirits", I said lowly, unable to gather the energy to speak in a normal tone. "Help me Spirits. I cannot do this on my own", and I dropped my head and closed my eyes. Then there was a voice, near me or within my head, my voice or another's I could not tell, but it said one word three times, and then was gone: "Remember". Slowly raising my head, looking towards the distance I concentrated on the word. Without thinking, I closed my eyes, emptied my mind and waited for a memory to come into view. It didn't take long. My dream of the old buck in the shelter of two trees waiting for the warmth of the sun returned to mind. Weather worn trees shaped by the winds blowing up from the valleys below, two trees on the east side of the mountain top, and a goat path running below with an outcropping of rock just beyond and above became once again clear. This was familiar. I had seen this before several times in these last few days. I thought it was just a short distance off. Was this a sign given to me or just my mind remembering the previous day while dreaming? My enthusiasm had returned quickly, so quickly that the change shocked me into further thought. Wasn't I excited and boastful in thought when I first started, and self-assured when there were fresh tracks to follow? Didn't I fail both times? This time I would go slowly; if being led I would follow. If the buck was there, it was being given to me. I would take what I had learned in this hunt and if there was more to learn, I would learn it. Maybe in that I would find what it was to be a man."

"With those thoughts in my mind, I picked up my bow and quiver and headed to the trees that were a short distance off. The air was calm as the first rays of the sun hit the mountain side. Small birds were flitting about, insects buzzing, and an occasional marmot whistled as I approached the trees from above. Slowly I crept, being as silent as I could, keeping to the larger rocks that stuck out past the trees where there was a view slightly above the goat path. Seeing a cleft between two large rocks, I peered over and looked down. There he was, a huge buck. His size spoke of years of climbing the rocks on this hillside. Scars of many past battles marked his hide, and a broken horn on his right side marked him as the aim of my quest. My heart pounded; this was what I had envisioned these past few days. The buck was no longer an idea in my head, he was real and now ready to die for my entrance into manhood. Slowly, as quietly as I could, I fitted an arrow into my bow, pulled back and aimed. Then a thought, let me drink in this moment, look closely to remember everything so to have the story to tell. Holding that pose, I focused on my prey, and saw something odd. Though he was big, his skin hung loosely over his muscles. He was old and had lost the tone of youth. Looking closer, he swayed as if struggling to stay upright and shivered from the cold as he waited for the rays of the sun to warm him. Then I saw his eyes, sad pools of darkness, age weighed heavily down upon him and the hurt of time could be seen through those eyes and it reached to a sad soul. To see what had once been such a mighty animal worn down by time stabbed at my soul. Such sorrow I felt for him. And then he sensed my presence, by instinct he stiffened up as if to fight or fly, but he just stood there. I knew he knew there was nothing to flee for. Escape me and the slow death he was living would soon overtake him. I felt for him, this once proud animal, standing there, weakened by age. Feeling the pain of his years, he was losing the will to live. I let my arrow fly, a good hit. He stood there for a moment, not flinching from the impact, then dropped to his knees. A calmness overcame him like no other animal that I had ever shot. He looked relieved, and then he fell over and was with his fathers."

"Everything started to go blurry, tears welled in my eyes, the passing of a great animal touched my soul; but even more so was the sadness I felt at his suffering, the torment of age upon that weakened frame. I went down and looked upon him and saw that my arrow had been a gift in ending his pain. Was this the end to all those of strength and endurance, was this what was in store for me if I became the man I envisioned myself to become, survivor of battles yet fallen by the curse of old age? The world looked differently now; the rite of manhood had changed me in a way I could never have imagined. The Spirits had done their work and set me on the path of being a man."

"He deserved a burial, this mighty old buck, so after taking his horns, I made a platform in a nearby tree. With my blanket I carefully wrapped his body and managed to get him up on the platform where I secured him the best I could. Though it might seem strange to give a goat the burial of a man, he had taught me much those few days that I hunted him. He deserved no less. It was a good way for him to end his life, to fall after evading a stronger enemy for many days. What he could not win by strength he nearly won by stealth, cunning, and endurance. He had gone to his fathers, proud of his accomplishment and I came back to the tribe humbled now knowing there was much more to become a true man than I had imagined."

Little Bear had questions to ask. He had never heard this story before and wanted to understand its meanings, but before he could speak Rolling Thunder stepped forward. Little Bear had not heard him approach and was a bit startled.

"I remember the day you came back," Rolling Thunder said with a smile. "You entered camp with strength in your step, bearing those horns with reverence. The boastful pride of youth purged from your soul allowing the man in you to start to grow."

Long Cloud was not surprised by Rolling Thunder's presence. As a good hunter/warrior is always aware of his surroundings, he had heard him approach earlier. Rising to his feet, nodding in respect he replied, "My quest taught me much and prepared me for many more lessons that I was to learn."

Little Bear could tell these words were intended for him as they continued. "And much more did you learn Long Cloud, I hope you too Little Bear will come back with a vision that starts you on the path of manhood." Long Cloud, as if with some signal, silently bowed out of their presence leaving them alone.

Little Bear was nervous as this was an honor to be in the sole presence of Rolling Thunder, to have his attention focused on you. This was a sign of entering manhood. Rolling Thunder looked like a kindly grandfather, weathered yet strong, kind eyes and a relaxed smile that had nothing but good will in them. As Chief, the whole tribe was his charge. All were his children, and this could be seen in his eyes as he looked proudly upon Little Bear as if looking at his own son. Little Bear had not noticed this before. Rolling Thunder was usually busy and did not directly interact with the youth of the tribe, but he was never short or sharp with them and often smiled when seeing the children happily playing. Rolling Thunder motioned to his supplies. "Bring them with you, Black Eagle awaits us and then you must be off."

Little Bear slung his quiver and bundle over his shoulder and with bow in hand walked beside Rolling Thunder towards the north side of camp. By now the camp was waking up as the last of the stars faded from view. Cooking fires were being rekindled, water and wood gathered. The tribe was a stir with activity. As Little Bear and Rolling Thunder passed people there were big smiles that stood out. A few children and friends of Little Bear fell in behind keeping a respectful distance, but trying to be close enough to hear any word they could. Little Bear felt embarrassed by the crowd of children that followed as if it was a reflection of him still being a child, but at the same time enjoyed being the center of attention. This conflict of mind troubled Little Bear, shouldn't he have new thoughts now that he had entered manhood? Shouldn't there be a night and day difference from who he was as a youth and who he was now as a man? With that uncertainty of mind came the fear that maybe he wasn't ready to become a man yet. Maybe he was still just a young boy who had pushed his way through the ceremonial flames into a rite before his time had come. With all this confusion going on in Little Bear's mind, Rolling Thunder was smiling to himself with the thought that the tribe, his family, was healthy. The crowd behind them with their jostles and giggles was music to his ears.

"Little Bear," Rolling Thunder said as the followers fell in behind, "today you start a scarce journey from which you will return changed, how so we do not know but changed you will be. The quest is not beyond what you can accomplish, the days may seem long, the nights cold, but these will pass. You are to go to Spirit Mountain, a three-day journey from here. The trail there will split at its base going in either direction. Follow the westward trail for a short distance and you will soon come upon a large flat rock at the base of a ridge rising to the northwest. There is an old little used trail that begins behind the rock. Follow this trail upwards and in half a day you will come to a small lake no more than a bowshot in length. Slightly above it is a recess into the mountain about two arm lengths deep that has a raised landing just outside of it. Make your camp there, it offers some protection. A small fire would be hidden from view, and from the landing you can sit looking out over the lake and wait for the Spirits to speak. You are to stay there until the Spirits speak all they have to say. Keep an eye out as you look over and into the lake. Listen carefully as they choose their own method to speak. How they will talk to you we cannot tell. After you have heard them, wait until the following morning to return, but keep on listening in case they have more to reveal. When you arrive back here you will meet with the council and we will discuss all that you have seen and heard."

"Be careful as you will be in the lower range of the Yarric. As you know, we have little to do with them and they are not friendly towards us. Six summers ago, they raided a hunting camp of ours. Two of their warriors died in that effort and they surely have not forgotten. If you are seen, they might seek revenge with your life so tread lightly and keep any fire small and unseen."

Little Bear was taking all of this in with great awe, these instructions were more difficult than any that he had heard given to the friends that had gone before him and the extent of them surprised him if not invoked a bit of fear. To go out several days from the camp was a test of his courage, but to enter the realm of the Yarric by himself stunned him, the thought of which challenged his nerve. The rite of manhood was never thought of as easy but this was more than stretching of one's courage; this rite could end in capture or death.

They now saw Black Eagle standing at the edge of the village looking north at the mountains in the distance. He stood unmoving, a solitary figure with the first rays of the sun just touching him. Three of the council members sat nearby, quietly talking over a small cooking fire. Long Cloud was nowhere to be seen. They came up within a few strides of Black Eagle and stopped without a word. After a moment of silence Black Eagle spoke without turning towards them.

"It is good to see you this morning Little Bear," then he paused. The council members rose, came over and stood to Little Bear's right side with the sun to their backs which seemed to cause their outline to glow in the morning light. The small crowd that followed, which now included Red Bird and her close friends, stood a few paces back not wanting to miss any part of the ceremony. They were antsy with excitement yet became quiet as soon as Black Eagle spoke.

Black Eagle slowly turned round and faced Little Bear, his eyes were of one deep in thought, his relaxed stance was that of one longing to go on an adventure but who accepted the fact that he could not. Briefly looking behind Little Bear, he smiled with contentment at the little crowd. This is how it should be, he thought. Close friends and family excited to see one of their own on his way to become a man, this was a healthy tribe. As he brought his eyes to Little Bear, it was with the look of a father releasing his son to stand on his own feet, to make his own decisions, to be a man of his own and no more the little child under his wing. Little Bear wondered at this having expected to see solemn reverence for the ceremonial rite of manhood, an event so excitedly waited for by a young boy of the tribe. This confusion of preconceived ideas to what he was seeing showed on his face which did not escape Black Eagle's eyes.

"This is a joyous event Little Bear, a special time in your life and the life of the tribe," he said with a warm smile. "The Spirits are looking down and seeing us happily putting you into their hands. They are intertwined in our lives, wanting to be treated with respect but not so much so that we only interact with them in ceremony. Like a father who loves and cares for his little children, so they are to us. As you go out on your quest, you are going out from under the care of the tribe and will be fully in the care of the Spirits. It is they who will give you guidance as you face your quest alone."

Black Eagle paused a moment to let his words soak in, this was not the time for long words so these few would give Little Bear concepts to think of on his quest. Continuing in a warm manner, "You know where you are going, though not what you will find. This is like life, following a certain direction into the future, but not knowing what the future holds." Another pause, Black Eagle smiled and noticed the proud face of Red Bird beaming with pride as she stood a few paces behind her son, like a mother bird seeing her fledgling taking off on its first flight. Near her stood White Fawn looking in admiration as her friends giggled at her. Few things were missed by Black Eagle. White Fawn's eyes for Little Bear were not one of them. Seeing her here was a sign that she planned on snaring Little Bear before one of the other young girls could. The hunter had become the prey, Black Eagle thought, and when he is totally ensnared, Little Bear will think he has done the catching, which made him smile the more. Black Eagle looked back to Little Bear and continued, "On your quest observe all, listen with a searching ear, and do not limit what you see to what you expect. Be open to the Spirits in any way they may speak to you. They speak with the word of man, bird, and animal; they speak with the wind blowing in the grass and trees, or the insect on its flight. They speak through the ripples on still water, the flames leaping in a fire, the stars and moon traveling overhead. Listen for them in the rocks falling from a mountain side, the groaning of the earth on a hot sunny day, a quiet voice in the recess of your mind. They will speak. Remember all you see and hear and we will search it out on your return."

With that said, Black Eagle, with calmness in his every move, glanced back to the mountains, and then turned walking back to his tepee. Rolling Thunder came and placed his right arm around Little Bear's shoulder, pointing towards the trail that led to Spirit Mountain. His arm was firm, firmer than the limbs of the friends he wrestled with. Hard as a tall tree yet it invoked a comfort, the expression of a father there to protect his child. "There is the path you must follow, from the first step upon it until you return is your quest. Keep wary of both man and animal, though the Spirits will be with you, the world can still bring you harm. Remember, the Spirits may speak as you first set out, while you wait upon them at the mountain, or on your trip home. Be alert as if you are stalking game, always aware, looking for sign, ever ready to listen, and your success will be a great boon to you and to the tribe."

With that, Rolling Thunder released his hold and stepped back two paces. This was a great moment; the firmness of Rolling Thunder's grip was gone and that made Little Bear light on his feet. Being freed from the Chief's arm was like being released from a fetter. Freedom called from the space ahead of him. Little Bear lept forward, bundle across his back, bow in hand, and sprinted to the trail that led into a sparsely populated wood. He did not look back, did not notice his mother's tears, did not hear the cheers of his friends behind. An inner force was driving him forward into an expanse of a wonderful unknown that was opening up to him; he was now a man set free.

To those left standing it was an exciting moment, seeing the transition of the Little Bear they knew into Little Bear the man, Little Bear the brave. The mothers watching had a kinship with Red Bird and shared in the joy as if it were their son. The young boys were proud to see their friend progress into manhood and dreamed of their turn to start their own quest. The young girls were impressed to see their friend be treated like a man by the council, admired his strength in body and spirit. White Fawn had a longing of heart, a desire for Little Bear the man to come back to her. The men watching first saw themselves on the beginning of their quests and strained to grasp once again the excitement they once had on that day long ago. Slowly they all turned back into camp to begin a normal day with unique dreams brought about by Little Bear's quest.

CHAPTER 4 - NORTH TO SPIRIT MOUNTAIN

Little Bear sprinted onto the path and into the trees, not noticing the bundle on his back, the bow in his hand, or the feel of the trail under his feet. He just ran as if the winds were carrying him and an unknown force was pulling him forward. In a little while, as if coming out of a dream, he found himself in an easy lope along the path that he knew well. Looking from side to side he soon became orientated with where he was and continued on at this easy pace until he came to a slightly open area with an outcropping of rocks just to the side of the trail. Little Bear slowed down and stopped, breathing hard he rested a moment while glancing to the rocks, the trail behind, and then back to the rocks. This was where his mother had told him she had hid a small pouch of dried meat to aide him on his quest. Little Bear had told her he did not want it, that he wanted to be true to his quest but his mother insisted saying all the mothers hid extra provision for their sons' quests and that he would need it before his quest was over. He planned on just leaving it, to not cheat thereby not diminishing his rite, but now the thought of being hungry came to mind. Running would build up an appetite and his rations would soon run out. Little Bear looked around again. Who would know, he thought. It seemed he could smell fresh buffalo cooking over a fire, memories of many fine meals came to mind. Then as if awaking from a dream, he spoke to the food that was calling him. "I would know!" There was quiet from the shock of his sudden outburst, quiet as in the calm after a storm.

With that, Little Bear turned to the path without further thought and started walking along the trail, past the rock outcropping and into the wood. Suddenly, without a sound, out from behind a tree stepped Long Cloud. Little Bear jumped back raising his bow and instinctively reaching for an arrow before he realized who it was before him.

"Long Cloud," he said with a slight gasp while lowering his bow, "I did not hear you."

"One must be constantly aware of their surroundings, ready for the unexpected and able to interpret and react at any time." Long Cloud's eyes were intense, more watchful than usual and this made Little Bear uneasy.

Now that the initial shock of Long Cloud's appearance was fading, the question coming to mind was why Long Cloud was here. Was this an accidental meeting or was he being watched on his quest? Little Bear was about to ask when Long Cloud spoke up.

"You did not take the food that is hidden back there."

Little Bear was surprised, how did he know of it? Did his mother tell him? Was this part of a test? An avalanche of thoughts were coming to mind and in the confusion of possibilities he stiffened up, felt threatened, and spoke out quickly with a harsh voice.

"The food is not mine; I did not put it there, so I did not take it!" A look of defiance came across Little Bear, feeling a bit guilty for even thinking of taking the food. He was going to protest with the pretense that he was far above this by being indignant.

Long Cloud was quick to see through the air Little Bear was putting on and knew he had to calm the situation before Little Bear got so worked up that he would neither listen nor hear what he had to say. "I know your mother put it there last night as most mothers do," responded Long Cloud. He had added the part about most mothers to head off any defensive attitude on his mother's behalf.

"And you thought I would take it, is that why you left it there

43

and were spying on me, to catch me cheating on my quest?" retorted Little Bear, still feeling he needed to defend himself.

Calmly, without averting his gaze, Long Cloud continued, "I had faith that you would not violate the trust we put in you, and you proved that by leaving it behind. Know this, when I came upon Red Bird hiding the food, an opportunity was opened to see better who you are. The council watches everyone to know them. When in battle you must know not only your enemy but also the brave by your side. Will he stand true in the heat of battle? Will he flinch or will he run away? In a hunt, what will he do if the buffalo turn towards you? You must act together; you must know what he is doing even if you cannot see him. You must know if you can trust him."

Little Bear started to interrupt but Long Cloud raised his hand to silence him. "I knew you would not take the food, but that is not what I was watching for, it was for how you did not take it."

Little Bear's face now showed puzzlement. Long Cloud saw this and it put his heart at ease. Little Bear was listening and trying to understand. The conflict was over; now was the time to teach.

"There are different ways to leave this food. Each would speak to who you are. If you ran past without giving a look, either your memory and ability to read signs are not good or you have a prideful heart and do not even want to associate with wrong. If you stopped and looked around and then continued, it could be curiosity or just considering the possibilities, advantages and disadvantages of taking the food. If you went over pulled it out, looked at it, then put it back, this would show that you were tempted and had not made up your mind as to what you would do before you got to this point. In all these possible scenarios, how you stand and the look on your face would speak to your intent and the struggles going on in your heart."

Little Bear was silent, no longer defensive; he was considering what Long Cloud said, trying to fully see things as Long Cloud saw them. There was no question that Long Cloud spoke the truth and this explanation left lots to think about. Little Bear had tried to read intent in others before, but never to this level, to see so many possibilities from a simple event. There was much to learn in becoming a man and much more to learn to be like Long Cloud. Long Cloud did not miss the change in Little Bear. No longer was he standing stiff and on edge, but was more relaxed in body with an expression that told of a mind piecing together a puzzle. This was good. Now was the time to retreat before more questions could be asked.

"I must go and you too have a long road ahead of you," Long Cloud said in his firm manner but with an edge of softness carefully spoken so not to renew Little Bear's defensiveness. "Remember you are on your own except for the Spirits watching over you. Look for small game and any wild food you come upon, sooner rather than later so that your rations do not run out."

Little Bear was about to ask a question but Long Cloud paid no attention and walked right past him and down the trail towards camp. It was useless to try and stop him, so Little Bear turned back to his quest and walked quickly along the path with many things to think about. Not noticed was that Long Cloud, upon rounding a corner and going a little past, listened, stopped, and turned back. With the stealth of a cougar, he followed Little Bear keeping far enough back to be neither seen nor heard.

Little Bear knew he had a lot of time to think over the recent events. The trail was long and each time it came to a clear rise the snow capped mountains in the distance looked far away and lonely. Keeping on the trail was easy; though not overly used, it ran pretty straight with occasional markers to guide searchers from ages past. Little Bear's first concern was not losing the trail as it became less pronounced the further he went from the tribe.

The tribe was now camping on the northern end of the prairies and rarely used this part of the woods. Some two summers before they had made camp in a small ravine a little farther north and to the west of the trail. This was the farthest north that Little Bear could remember and he thought it would be good to see their old camp. Being narrow with steep walls on either side, it would make an easy hunt to catch any game that happened to be within while satisfying his curiosity as to what the old camp looked like now.

The sun was high overhead when Little Bear reached a side trail that led into the ravine. Notching an arrow to his bow, Little Bear put himself into the mindset of a hunter with ears on edge and an eye that searched for fresh animal sign or movement amongst the trees and brush, and then slowly edged his way forward. The ravine was about two bow shots wide and ten deep with sheer side walls twice as high as the tallest pine tree that grew within. Large and small rock had fallen over the years which piled up at the bottom of the walls, giving lots of hiding places that the young children played in back when the tribe camped here. The floor of the ravine was mostly flat with an occasional boulder among the sparse trees, brush, and poison oak. Little Bear remembered the poison oak from when they camped here before. Too many times he stumbled into it and suffered days of relentless itching. A small creek ran through the ravine most of the year which flowed from a spring near the back wall. Next to the spring was a narrow path built into the wall that climbed to the butte above. This was the only other way out besides the mouth of the ravine.

Little Bear slowly stalked his way in, careful to make no noise, using the cover that was available, intently aware of his surroundings. There was an old trail that ran back to a clearing where the tribe once camped near the rear of the ravine. Memories drew him back into the time past when they once camped in this same spot. Some of the larger rocks that had broken off the cliffs and bounded into the ravine looked familiar, bringing visions of the past playing with his friends among and atop the boulders. With each step more memories came in: the sounds of friends laughing, the warm sun shining through the trees, the aroma of cooking fires and the flavor of fresh buffalo. Little Bear was enjoying these memories when there was a movement that caught his eye, he froze. Half a bowshot away, moving slowly amid shafts of light that angled through the trees, was a young deer. Moving a few steps at a time, unaware of Little Bear's presence, it was enjoying the fresh spring leaves on a clump of blackberry vines. Little Bear slowly brought his bow to bare down on his intended prey, a good prize this early in the quest with enough meat to last many days. He chose the spot for his arrow to hit; but he did not let his arrow fly. Relaxing his bow, he thought of the waste. Too much meat to carry when he needed to travel light. It would not be right to kill any creature and leave any of its flesh to rot in the open. This was not the way of the tribe; the Spirits would not be pleased. Turning back to the path that led to the clearing, he stalked on knowing there would be plenty of small game to be had.

It did not take long for Little Bear to reach the clearing, stopping as he came to the edge of the trees to survey what lay ahead. Brush was moving in where tepees once stood and old fire rings could still be discerned as could a few paths through the overgrown grass. Time was erasing the memory of their camp from the land. How long would it be until all traces of the camp were gone and the only remembrances of it would be in his mind, and even that would one day be gone. Little Bear's mind drifted back seeing this camp when it was alive, fires blazing, the tribe busy with life and echoes bouncing off the walls; then the empty space before him came back into view along with a silence that magnified the emptiness. How many other camps were disappearing, lost to all memory? This thought made Little Bear feel small, like an insect about to be swallowed up in a moment, just a bug eaten by a robin that then goes off in search of other prey giving no thought to the morsel it just ate. A sadness started to creep into his heart, these memories would soon disappear like his childhood, and those joyful times were fading as his new life as a man began. Little Bear's eyes now began to see only rocks, trees, brush and the sky as the memories disappeared. I am a child no more he said to himself, and turned back to his quest.

Emerging out of the ravine, Little Bear followed the path at a light trot with the intent to make up time lost in his little detour. At first, he felt he sounded like a buffalo running down the path. He heard each foot fall, the arrows jostling against each other in his quiver, his bag bouncing on his back; but soon he began to ignore these sounds which were much quieter than he believed, and the sounds of the woods was all that he heard. Bees buzzed, small birds flitted about as Little Bear jogged down the path, and always the mosquitoes were ready to bite when going through a cool damp area. Every stream was a stop to quench his thirst, refill the small water skin that was in his bundle, and an opportunity to wet his hair and cool off a little before starting off again. The warm excitement of the adventure drove Little Bear on while youth and an active life provided the strength and endurance to maintain his pace.

As the shadows were lengthening with the approach of evening, Little Bear became more attentive. Though not deep woods, darkness would come quickly and a secure place to camp needed to be found. Coming over a slight rise, the deep throb of wings surprised him as a couple of grouse noisily leapt up and flew into a nearby tree. Grouse, not being the smartest of birds, provided an easy target and a large one soon fell to Little Bear's arrow.

With bird in hand, it was but a few minutes down the path to where a small stream crossed. Retreating a little way back and slightly above the trail, a level area behind a few rocks was found that offered cover from view for a small fire and camp. Putting his supplies and bird aside, Little Bear quickly gathered a small supply of dry wood from a broad area so as not to have the area look like it was picked clean for a nearby camp. After stacking the wood in a convenient pile, next was to build a small fire ring within easy reach of the wood. The ground was dug out a little, saving the dirt to cover the fire's remains in the morning. It did not take long to now kindle a fire and prepare the grouse to be cooked.

Yarric territory was near, but far enough away to cook a meal without great fear of being found. Caution was best so Little Bear kept his fire low and with little smoke, slowly roasting his grouse to the side of the flames to keep any juices from disturbing the fire. The grouse had been cut into several smaller pieces and skewered so that they could be positioned closer to the flames and cooked more evenly. As the bird slowly sizzled, its savory aroma brought Little Bear's appetite out, a smile grew with the satisfaction of his first day into manhood that included this tasty meal. Alone for the first time so far from camp he had traveled on his own toward a hostile territory with no sense of fear. Excitement in the hunt earlier in the day had helped him to now focus on the change in his status, and then obtaining the grouse, providing his own meal, helped him feel that he could survive on his own. No thought of what it was to be a man came to mind. Little Bear just enjoyed the moment along with the anticipation of the soon to be eaten grouse.

It seemed to take forever but finally the smaller pieces were ready. Taking a skewer of meat, its hot juices stung Little Bear's lips as he hungrily bit into it. Some lessons must be learned repeatedly. Acting impulsively when hungry had its consequences. Now carefully blowing on each piece, not only was it safe to bite into, but the aroma filled his lungs and added to the pleasure of the meal. It tasted so good, having been caught by his own hand, cooked in his fire built by his hand, and satisfying the hunger of a day long run. This meal filled both mind and body.

As Little Bear's hunger was slowly being quenched, he watched the flames dance in his little fire, and this brought back the memory of the flames he had walked through the night before. The whole tribe was assembled for him, watched him walk through the ceremonial flames as he approached the council. Now here he was by a little fire eating his grouse alone.

Looking up between the trees he could see that night had fallen and the stars were shining brightly. He had heard many stories of how his ancestors were up among the stars. Somehow that was not very comforting as he sat there alone so far from home. The contrast was great: a raging fire with the whole tribe about and now alone with the possibly of the Spirits of the dead

49

looking down upon him and his little fire. Little Bear could hear the creatures of the night in the woods and it evoked a kind of fear that he had not known. There seemed to be an emptiness in the woods, something without form that was on the prowl, something that would swallow him whole. Pulling his knees close to his chest after the last bite of his evening meal, he slowly rocked back and forth feeling small, hoping he was so small that he would be overlooked by whatever was lurking about.

Was it a mistake to enter the rite of manhood, Little Bear questioned. Was he too young? Would a man have these fears? Shouldn't he think and feel something different from the time before the start of the rite? Now there came a host of questions as to what it was to be a man. Was it a sudden change or did you grow into it? Were you taught or did you just naturally grow into manhood? Could you see it on the outside or was it on the inside? Little Bear looked back, tried to remember other members of the tribe as they approached and entered manhood, but no memory came that answered the questions that haunted him. Looking back to when he approached Long Cloud about wanting to go through the rite of manhood, Long Cloud stood there in his stoic way listening, his eyes reading him like reading sign on a hunt, taking in everything while not giving a hint of what his thoughts were. Little Bear wondered what Long Cloud saw that made him agree that he was ready to become a man. Long Cloud's judgment was always trusted, but was he right this time? Little Bear no longer felt the emptiness as he as he was too engrossed in his thoughts and with unanswered questions. Putting a few heavy sticks on the fire and pulling the buffalo skin tightly, he lay down close to the fire and entered a fitful sleep.

Morning came along with the stiffness of a long run and a cold night of sleeping on the forest floor. Opening his eyes, Little Bear could see the skies lightening up beyond the sparse treetops of open forest. Slowly rising to his feet, cautiously he peered around and seeing no sign of human life, stretched out his complaining muscles. The cool morning air gave him a shiver, so draping the buffalo skin about his shoulders, Little Bear bent down over the fire pit and breathed life back into the embers, adding a few more small sticks to the now growing flames. It did not take long to warm the leftover grouse to provide another warm meal. Strange, Little Bear thought, it did not taste as succulent as it did the night before. It was a bit dry but that was not it. It did not evoke any memories, no thoughts like the night before. There was a mystery here, but one to be solved later for the day was beginning and the desire to be off was starting to grow.

After finishing his meal, Little Bear rolled up his buffalo skin, buried the remains of the grouse, and hid the evidence of the camp. Now was the time to be careful as hostile territory was near and caution was a necessity. Taking a few steps back to look where he had spent the night, no trace could be found.

With a smile of self-satisfaction, Little Bear turned and headed back to the trail and then the short distance to a little stream that crossed the path. Glancing around first, he washed in the cold water that brought shivers to fully wake him. The morning was cool enough but the water stung as the grime of the night was washed away. Now every nerve seemed alive and screamed "no more!" The sound of the water splashing on the rocks was crisp and assailed his ears. After refilling the water skin and securing his supplies on his back, Little Bear started north again on the path of manhood; the Spirits awaited.

Slowly at first, reacquainting himself with the trail, keeping an eye and ear open for any sign of hostile life, he walked. Within a few moments his pace picked up to a quick walk, the stiffness of night and the cool morning were receding as muscles warmed from the exercise. The cool air no longer penetrated as Little Bear moved into a gentle lope. How good it felt to glide along the trail, passing through the shadows as the morning sun fingered its way between tree and branch to light his way.

Steadily, Little Bear ran on. His attention alternated between being aware of his surroundings and trying to catch every glimpse of the mountain ahead as it came into view. Slowly it grew. At first it seemed far but by midday it could be seen clearly. Snow capped the top half, which was more rounded than a peak, and shown brightly with the clear blue sky behind. The path dipped into a little bowl, thereby offering a more unobscured view of the mountain ahead. Little Bear paused for a brief rest and used this opportunity to look upon his goal. Close he thought, close enough to be reached that day, a day sooner than Rolling Thunder had thought. He took in a deep breath; pride filled him as he imagined what the council would think of his making this trek to Spirit Mountain in only two days; how impressed they would be. Truly he was a man now.

Taking out his water skin and a small piece of dried meat to have a quick meal before continuing, Little Bear thought about how far he had traveled, how far he was from the tribe. Looking back over his shoulder and not recognizing the area, he felt alone, vulnerable. A small bird moved in the brush not far from his side. He jumped. All his senses were on edge as he slowly looked around, hearing the occasional movement of a bird, the buzzing of an insect, the breeze flowing through the trees. Then there was the mountain, no longer a beautiful snow capped high hill but an ominous cold rock with Spirits upon its flanks waiting for him. A cold shudder ran down his back; pride and confidence vanished like the light of day as the sun dips below the far-off horizon. Little Bear stepped back against a nearby pine, finding a bit of security by the solidness of its trunk. Staring at the mountain, his heart sank. To face a charging buffalo would be easier than this mountain that looked as cold as death.

Now that thought came, did he have to go? Who would know if he went no further? If he was found out, who would blame him? Who would be willing to face the Yarric and the Spirits so far from home?

An eagle screeched and broke the trance that had gripped him. Little Bear's full attention was on the bird as it soared overhead. The shock of that cry pushed all other thoughts out of his head which was soon filled with marvel as it soared effortlessly through the skies. Without a flap of a wing the eagle circled, caught an updraft, and rose higher and higher in full control of the skies. Little Bear watched, no longer seeking the strength of a tree, but standing erect watching this lone eagle soar far from its nest. With each breath he now took, strength and confidence came flowing in. Courage returned as he shared a comradery with the eagle that soared in the empty skies alone, holding itself up no matter what was ahead. Quickly replacing the water skin, hoisting the bundle and quiver to his back and setting his resolve to face whatever lay ahead, Little Bear set off with a new determination, unaware that he was being observed from behind.

Long Cloud was following with a sharp eye and ear, keeping far enough behind to be unseen but close enough to see. Seeing how observant Little Bear was might come later if someone else were about. Long Cloud had to be close enough to spot him and to see how Little Bear reacted. As for his not seeing Long Cloud, few could spot him if he did not wish it. The pace had been better than anticipated, endurance complimenting strength, which spoke well of Little Bear. So far Little Bear had done well; treading quietly, obscuring his camp where few could find traces, providing his own meal, these were good signs of a boy becoming a man.

Reading this latest scene was not difficult. Little Bear had confronted the reality of where he was. His sudden looking back followed by recoiling from what was ahead showed that he was thinking and the fears of youth were taking hold. It would have been nice to see Little Bear overcome these without the prompting of the eagle, master fear without any help, yet this could also be a sign of his listening to the Spirits, a good sign indeed.

The trail stretched on, slowly climbing as it followed the contours of the foothills leading up to the mountain. Now being in Yarric territory Little Bear had to be more cautious, slowing down at every bend to ensure he would not burst into a hunting party or chancing upon a lone messenger. The trail was not well used which gave some comfort, yet how long would this last? If only the whereabouts of the Yarric camps were known, it would be easier to guess the chances of running across someone.

With the slowing of pace, the lake could not be reached that night. Accepting this, Little Bear pulled an arrow from the quiver so to be ready for any small game and increased his awareness to once again add to his provisions. Running most of the day built up a large appetite and it would not be satisfied easily. Pausing to hunt a chanced upon animal was possible. Game could be taken if in the process the Yarric did not find him. Little Bear decided not to stop and hunt but only be ready if by chance he saw an animal. Better to reach the mountain. Upon its flanks above the main trail where none would be passing he could hunt there where there was less chance of being the prey instead of the hunter.

Shadows were now stretching long as the air started to cool, it would soon be time to seek a place of shelter for the night. Rounding a large boulder, the trail jutted up a steep incline to what looked like a broad shelf. Stopping for a moment to let his heavy breathing subside and scan for any movement, Little Bear saw the mountain rise up before him making a clean break from the foothills below. Cautiously ascending the shelf, peering over the top before committing to reveal himself, he looked carefully each way, listened, and then climbed up to get his bearings. A heavily used trail met him going east and west, it bowed out to a point where the trail he had been following rose up to meet it. From here the trail going south was seen disappearing quickly into the trees thereby letting Little Bear know he had not been seen from this point. Looking to the Southwest and seeing the sun was low, told that night would soon come, time was short.

Turning west, Little Bear set off with his ears straining, eyes searching as far up as the trail allowed. A well-worn trail was easier to follow but he would be more likely be found by the Yarric. Fortunately, it only took a few moments to come across a small stream with a large rock to the side of the path. Quickly filling his water skin again, Little Bear searched and easily found a very old trail that looked unused behind the rock. A sense of relief filled him knowing that this was the path Black Eagle spoke of and that he was on track to complete his quest.

The shadows were very long now, daylight soon to be exhausted. To try and follow the trail even on a moonlit night was foolish, too easy to get lost or twist an ankle in the dark. Going about two bow shots up the trail was a small group of rocks that offered some protection, a good place to spend the night. Little Bear quickly gathered some dry wood and arranged a fire pit next to the rocks opposite to the trail. As he prepared to kindle a fire there was a sound. Straining his ears, he heard a voice and soon the sound of foot falls upon the trail below and the occasional voice in a language he did not know. It was going to be a cold night as a fire could not be chanced, no telling how many others would pass him by before dawn came.

Looking at what supplies were left, one day's ration and a full skin of water, Little Bear slowly ate half while watching the skies darken. Half a day's travel up to the lake Black Eagle had said, a little longer if keeping an eye out for game he thought. There should be little chance of meeting a hunting party as Spirit Mountain was off the commonly used trails. If seen from below, as long as he could not be recognized as a member of the Kengeia tribe, he would be safe.

The Spirits were waiting; he wondered if they lived upon the mountain or came here just to speak to man. If this was true, how did they speak to Long Cloud on his quest or to Black Eagle at camp? Why did they tell Black Eagle for him to meet them here if they spoke to him the night of his rite? He could have heard them there and neither of them would have had to travel to this mountain. Many questions came to mind. Would they be answered by the Spirits or by Black Eagle? Pulling his buffalo skin tightly around him, getting as comfortable as possible, Little Bear closed his eyes without further thinking and was asleep in moments.

Birds chirped nearby startling Little Bear. His eyes opened

wide with astonishment that he had slept hard through the night and into the next morning. The sun, though low in the eastern sky, was shining brightly and offering its warmth after a cold night. The mountain air stung Little Bear's cheeks, the only part of him that poked out of the warmth of the buffalo skin. The previous day's travel took a bit out of him; it took a full night of sleep to recover. Slowly sitting up with a watchful eye, cold currents of the morning's air fingered their way in and stung the skin. Stiff muscles once again needed to be stretched in preparation for the day's hike, but right now the comfort of a warm buffalo skin was more alluring. Wrapping his cloak tightly about, Little Bear sipped water and ate half of what was left of the provisions.

There was soon nothing left to do but to stretch, gather the few possessions at hand, restore the campsite to show no sign of his passing, and head off up the trail in search of Spirit Lake and any game along the way. The mountain was alive with animals about their daily lives, even two deer feeding on fresh leaves with a fawn nearby. Onward Little Bear pressed, intently following the trail that often disappeared, reclaimed by the mountain for a time and then reemerging in its upward climb. As the sun climbed higher all sign of the east west trail that ran below was gone thereby removing the fear of being seen. Trees grew smaller in their stature, the ground became a harder, less fertile soil, the water colder from a nearby snowpack. Rounding a small ridge that rose from the southwest, a level area projected out where part of the mountain had slid down ages before. There, the light blue of a shallow lake lay, with a thin rim of green on its eastern side where a line of trees stood before the mountainside dropped off revealing open sky beyond.

CHAPTER 5 - THE LAKE

Little Bear smiled, and then laughed; he had found it. Small though it was, he had found it. He drank it in; the beauty of the scene being so much better having found it on his own. No thought of Spirits, no remembrance of the quest, the rite forgotten for the present, only the goal of the lake, and now obtaining the ledge above it lay before him.

Scanning the mountainside over the lake, Little Bear bound off in his final search for the ledge overlooking the lake. No longer following the trail, an occasional rock was knocked loose which would tumble down the gentle slope stopped by either brush or small outcropping of rock that populated the hillside. With the lake being small it did not take long to come across a small depression about two arm spans wide and just as deep.

It was tall enough to be able to stand in most of it without hitting one's head, and with its slightly sloping floor it was sure to keep dry if a rain did not blow in from the east. A little landing just outside the depression had a berm slightly more than knee high which would help conceal a small fire. There was an old small fire pit just under the upper lip of the depression, positioned as to not let its light be seen from either side or above though far enough forward to allow any smoke to freely get out. In the very back of the depression raised up on rocks was a store of dry wood that looked several years old. This had been used as a campsite before, but not in quite some time.

Carefully knocking the wood free to ensure no snakes or spiders were within, Little Bear neatly stacked the wood next to the fire pit estimating that two days' worth was ready to be used. Whether it was a traveler or someone on a spiritual journey who left the wood there, Little Bear did not know, but he appreciated finding it and vowed to leave a good supply when he left.

Picking up a small branch, Little Bear took his knife and whittled the branch down on one end to make a sharp spike, then taking a large stone he hammered it into the back wall making a peg to hold his bag of nearly depleted provisions. Stepping back with a look of satisfaction, Little Bear admired his new camp. To spend a few days there was not going to be as hard as he had once imagined. Turning around and stepping out to the low berm, he surveyed his new surroundings. The eastern sky showed a few clouds rolling by, their reflection in the little lake below. It was now time to restock the supplies. Though there might be fish to be had, marmot, fowl, or possibly a deer would be a better choice.

Little Bear slung his quiver over his shoulder and with bow in hand stood quietly with ear and eye keenly surveying the mountainside. A slight whistle could occasionally be head to the north, the whistle of a marmot. Not seeing any movement, he headed up and to the north to join the path which would be more stable to walk upon and thereby make less noise. In a short while traces of the old trail were found and easily followed. Stepping quietly, making use of whatever cover was available, Little Bear quickly crept along with his senses focused on the hunt.

Occasional berry bushes and vines looked promising but it was too early in the season for there to be ripe fruit. Small birds were fluttering about, not big enough to be worth trying to make a meal out of. The noise they made was welcomed as it helped disguise his presence. Unfortunately, traveling at this slower speed provided a feast for swarms of hungry insects. Little Bear resisted swatting at them except when they neared his eyes. What did they eat when he was not around he thought. His mind began to wander, thoughts of flying high like an eagle, above the insects, above the hard mountainside, to spy out the land and swoop down on young prey; that would be the way to hunt. Patience was not easy for a young man, especially a hungry one. Peering around each rock outcropping he started seeing visions, a buffalo, an elk, sometimes a deer and then the cooking fires with fresh meat slowly roasting. Hunting was hard on an empty stomach.

Stopping by a boulder that had become wedged between two trees, Little Bear took a drink from his water skin. He wondered if his wandering mind had caused him to miss an opportunity in his hunt. The mind is hard to control on an empty stomach, he thought. The sun had crested the mountain and everything was in the shade and slowly cooling down. Night was still far off yet being on the downside of the day gave cause to redouble his effort.

Peering around the tree to gain a view of where he was going, he saw movement. Just ahead and below the trail were two deer, yearlings, two young bucks with small spikes for antlers. They were slowly browsing, eating a few salal leaves, and then taking a couple of steps to try some tastier looking plants. Little Bear slipped back behind the trees and set his water skin down. Pulling out an arrow and fitting it to the bow, he pulled the string back and slowly stepped around the trees as smoothly as he could. He stood there aiming at the nearest deer and waited until both of their heads were down and searching for some delicate young leaf. His fingers released the arrow and it flew swiftly to its mark and sunk in. The shock of the arrow hitting stunned the buck, and it leaped forward wide-eyed wondering what hit him, but the shot was a good one, behind the shoulder and through the heart. His legs crumpled under him and he fell, in those few seconds life left him thereby ensuring Little Bear's life would continue. The remaining deer just stood there, not knowing what to do until Little Bear stepped forward and on hearing him, the buck jerked its head toward Little Bear and seeing him advancing, bounded off, disappearing from view in just a few leaps down a nearby gully.

Little Bear, with another arrow ready to fly, cautiously advanced to where the deer lay. Coming up to it and seeing there was no need for another shot, he eased up on his bow and admired his success. Though on the small side, this deer would last for many days, maybe even until his return to the tribe. Not a deer to be proud of if one were gauging hunting skills as it was young and not wise with age, but it would serve its purpose in sustaining him. As Little Bear looked upon the deer, the thought came that this was a live creature like himself; he breathed, ate, and lived upon the land. The deer's life was over so that Little Bear could live. How many more animals were to die so that he could live? In his mind's eye he saw a field full of bison, deer, squirrels, marmots, and a host of birds, all that were destined to give their lives for him. Little Bear did not like this vision, "Why should so many die that I might live?" he thought. Focusing once again on the deer he had just killed, Little Bear spoke: "You have died young my friend; your life has been given to me and I shall not waste it. You now shall live on within me, your flesh becoming my flesh. May your spirit go to your fathers knowing that you have fulfilled your purpose here. I will live a life that will bring honor to your sacrifice." Standing there, looking down upon the young buck, the wind could be heard as it blew past him. Its cold touch added to the thought of death that was now on his mind.

Knowing that time was short, Little Bear quickly field-dressed the deer and laid it on some nearby rocks so that the blood would flow out. Then going back to where his arrow lay, it was a valuable tool and not to be abandoned, he cleaned and inspected it for damage. It was still in good condition, a good omen. After placing the arrow in his quiver, Little Bear quickly covered the evidence of his hunt with moderate care. There was little chance of anyone coming this way but it was best to leave his passing not easily seen.

The afternoon was now getting on and there was a deer to get back to camp. Luckily, Little Bear had been traveling slightly uphill so, with a deer draped over his shoulder, his bow in hand, he started back. The way was more difficult with the extra weight that he bore. What was left of the trail offered little help in giving sure footing and Little Bear slipped several times and fell once. It seemed like a long time when he finally saw the landing in front of his camp. Sweat was rolling off his brow and he was sore from stumbling as he laid his prize upon the rocks inside the hollow of the hill which was to be his home for a time. The weight felt good coming off his shoulder; he felt so much lighter after packing the deer all that way down a rocky path.

After a long draft of cool water, Little Bear began the chores he had to get done before nightfall. First was refilling his water skin from the lake below, a short climb down a path that many had used before while staying at this same camp. He wanted to dive in and clean off all the dirt, blood, and sweat but night was near, time was scarce, and being wet at nightfall and only being able to make a small fire was dangerous. With his water skin full, he climbed back up the hill gathering several green branches and brought them to his camp.

The sky was now turning a deep blue with a few clouds that were red as a blazing fire. Being in the shadows on the east side of the mountain made it darker yet, and the coolness of the evening was creeping in as the warmth of the sun was long gone. With the dry wood in the recess, Little Bear quickly kindled a fire that brought warmth and needed light in his new little home. With no poles to suspend the deer from and any tree being too far from the fire, he skinned the deer as it lay across the rocks. Once complete, the large branches that he had just gathered were stripped bare and tied together with strips of the deer's hide to form a crude drying rack as was commonly done back at his camp. Now Little Bear went to work cutting the deer meat into thin strips and hung them over his rack. Several larger pieces of meat were left for roasting, a well-deserved meal after the work done this day and enough for several more days. Taking three sticks a little shorter than an arm's length, he stripped them of their bark and sharpened one end to hold his meal. When these three pieces of meat were skewered they were ready for roasting. They were seared in the flames to lock the juices within, and then set to slowly cook by the edge of the fire.

The moon had risen over the horizon and was lighting up

the mountainside, and when combined with the fire light, Little Bear's temporary home was well lit. The fire, smoke, and Little Bear's scent would keep most animals at bay even though the smell of the deer carcass would be tempting. Placing it near the edge of the landing and against the hillside, Little Bear covered the bones with a light layer of dirt to further hide its scent until morning when it could be safely dealt with. This being done, he put a little more wood on the fire to ensure it would last a little while untended, repositioned the skewered hunks of venison so they would not burn, rolled up the freshly skinned hide, and carefully made his way down the moonlit mountainside to the lake below. The hide was soon washed and laid across a nearby bush, then Little Bear cleaned himself up the best he could without getting too wet. The water stung as he rubbed his hands and arms to be rid of the blood and grime that was caked on him, it felt good to have his arms clean and it was tempting to wash his whole body, but the stiffness of the grime would have to be endured for a while as the cold-numbing water would chill him too much. The night would have to be passed in his present state as the bear blanket was not big enough to keep him warm if he was wet from this mountain lake.

Looking across the lake, Little Bear saw the reflection of the moon and stars on the water that was stretched before him. Light ripples made the stars dance on its surface and made Little Bear smile at the simple pleasure of enjoying its beauty. Then there was what looked like a mist or fine fog that slowly rolled over the water near the shore that was heading towards him. Little Bear soon realized that this was no mist but a cloud of mosquitoes that was heading his way, and they were hungry. Quickly grabbing the deer hide, Little Bear made his way back up to the fire and hoped this hungry hoard did not try to follow him.

As Little Bear approached his camp, he noted the flames of the fire could not be seen but its flickering red glow could be discerned against the mountain walls. Even though there would probably be no one nearby to see, caution was best. Taking the deer hide, Little Bear hung it on the overhead of the recess thereby trapping some of the glow within, being above the fire, the skin would also capture heat and aid its drying. Little Bear looked at this setup and felt pleased all was going well so far.

Pulling out his buffalo skin and draping it around his shoulders, Little Bear sat down facing the fire, his back to the mountainside. With a short stick, he stirred the fire bringing the coals together and then laid another piece of wood on the fire. Taking one of the skewers of meat, Little Bear tasted his evening meal and it was good. Fresh venison roasted on a fire, juices steaming within, its warmth filling his body with each bite, and all provided by his hand. Becoming a man seemed very fulfilling this night. Little Bear slowly ate, enjoying the moment as the sky darkened while he felt safe in his little camp on that lonely mountainside.

When he finished, the drying racks were checked so the meat would dry evenly. It was satisfying to see several days' worth of fresh meat drying, knowing hunger would be put off for a while. Little Bear arranged enough dry wood to be in easy reach to last the night. Putting a piece of wood on the fire, he looked about to see that his work was done, and then wrapping the buffalo skin tightly around himself, was soon asleep.

Outside a pair of eyes had been watching for some while. Long Cloud had never been far away, close enough to see, stealthy enough not to be seen. A master hunter, he had tracked Little Bear the entire way, occasionally seeing him a little way ahead, always aware of where he was. Reading the one you are tracking was important, and Long Cloud knew how to read the signs.

So far all had gone well. Long Cloud had seen when Little Bear faltered earlier on and then recovered himself. He watched as Little Bear pressed hard on his quest and what care he took to cover his camps. Little Bear could handle himself alone in the wild; he was now the young fledgling that was spreading his wings and flying high. Long Cloud felt proud, to see his nephew become a man as he took on his quest, to see the future of the tribe filled with strength; Long Cloud was pleased.

Now that Little Bear was settling into his surroundings, Long Cloud had to see to his own needs. Earlier in the day when Little Bear was hunting, Long Cloud was following a bit behind and above. Since Little Bear would be in this area for several days, some of which could entail hunting, every effort had to be made not to be seen and not to leave tracks that could be found. Little Bear would be cautious being in Yarric territory, but if he spotted a fresh moccasin print, he would be extra alert making it hard to keep close enough to observe him.

When Little Bear shot the deer, Long Cloud knew there was time for his own preparation. Going on ahead, a marmot was soon found and easily shot. With a marmot in hand and the day growing late, a camp needed to be set up before beginning an evening meal. Long Cloud's camp had to be far enough away not to be accidently found yet near enough that traveling back and forth would not take much time, and also be near its own source of water. A stream, more of a trickle, was found along with a protrusion of rocks that would serve well for cover. There was plenty of deadwood about, so Long Cloud quickly gathered enough to cook a meal to last a cold night through. Unlike Little Bear, Long Cloud would remove all traces of his camp each morning and then return in the evening; no chance was going to be taken on being discovered by the Yarric or Little Bear.

As night began to give way to morning, Long Cloud quickly concealed his camp, refilled his water skin, and made his way back towards Little Bear's camp. It was important to stay hidden yet have a clean view of Little Bear and his camp, thinking distance was best at first until Little Bear's movements and how he approached his quest were known. Long Cloud headed down the mountainside, then angled over and came up below and on the north side of the lake. From here he could stay hidden among the trees while peering out across the water to watch Little Bear's movements. Chances were, Little Bear would stay on his side of the lake and not force Long Cloud from his hiding place, and from this position the mountainside could be observed to see if any Yarric by chance might be in the area.

Little Bear awoke from a deep sleep, his fire now out and the chill of the morning creeping in. Sitting up it was disappointing to find a cold camp as he had anticipated waking up from time to time to feed the fire, but the previous day's exertion had taken its toll. Starting a warm fire was appealing but there were other priorities. First was the deer carcass which needed to be removed and hidden. Stiffly arising and stepping to the edge of the berm, Little Bear surveyed his surroundings. A little way to the north was an area that looked like it had recently had landslides, a place where the earth would be fairly loose and avoided by anyone traversing the mountainside. Laying the deer hide out, he uncovered the carcass and placed it on the deer hide. This being done, Little Bear made his way along the mountainside; he came across an area with loose earth and a fair amount of brush. Finding a short stick, he quickly dug a hole, buried the carcass, covering it up leaving the area looking undisturbed. Looking back to his camp, Little Bear felt reassured that if found by a bear or cougar, it was far enough away to keep him safe.

Rolling up the deerskin, Little Bear headed down to the lakeside to clean up. Once again, the deerskin was washed and set aside, and then Little Bear took the opportunity to bathe. Cold though the water was, it felt good to wash the grime from several days of physical activity. A little warmth could be felt from the first rays of the sun, but not enough to quell the shivering that racked his body. Climbing out of the water, Little Bear quickly rolled up the deerskin with shaking hands and headed back to camp with visions of starting a warm fire. It was a short climb up, grabbing a few more pieces of wood on the way, and the exertion helped cut the chill he was feeling.

Reaching camp, the buffalo skin quickly pulled around his shoulders, Little Bear kindled a fire making sure it remained as smokeless as possible. Hunched closely over the flames to get the most heat, he rubbed his hands and edged even closer enjoying the warmth this little fire offered. Staring at the little flames as they danced on the wood, Little Bear felt a calmness that seemed to flow from the fire to him and through him. Was the fire alive he mused; did it have a mind of its own? It could be warm and friendly, sharing its life-giving warmth, or raging hot with anger destroying all in its path. With its death, the cold of the grave would seem to pull at you with cold arms as its last flicker of life disappeared into black ash. Little Bear took a small piece of wood and held it out so that it just touched a flame. Slowly the little flame licked the edges of the wood, almost caressing it, until a new flame appeared on the wood which was held in his hand. Carefully lifting the wood and flame up, Little Bear watched the flame as it slowly grew. Was this flame alive? Little Bear pondered these questions as he moved the wood side to side to get a better view, being careful not to extinguish the little flame. "Are you alive?" he asked the little flame, but no answer came. Gently he placed the wood and flame back into the fire. With the soft words, "Go back to your parents," a smile came to Little Bear's face as he watched the surrounding flames dance with the little flame and then engulf the piece of wood. Visions of the dancing around a fire in camp came back to mind, happy memories of being with friends and family. Perhaps there was a kinship between the tribe and the fire, a tribe of man and a tribe of fire, both fought to survive side by side in this world. Glancing up, the morning sky held clouds that told of coming rains that were on their way. Looking back down to the fire, the flames looked unaware of their coming enemy. "Rest easy my little ones, you are safe with me for a while" Little Bear softly said as he added more wood to the fire.

As the fire hungered for wood, Little Bear also had a hunger that did not want to be ignored. Taking a few of the roasting sticks from the previous night, he skewered three pieces of fresh deer meat and set it to roasting by the fire. Looking at his stores, he saw there was enough fresh meat for two days, dried meat for a week, and a small amount left from what was brought along from camp. This was a satisfying sight. There was enough to last for the trip back to camp if the Spirits did not take long in revealing themselves. With these thoughts, Little Bear remembered the beginning of his quest and the extra food that his mom had hidden away for him to secretly take. A mixture of pride and shame came over him, pride that he had not given in to the temptation which he could now see he did not need, and shame that he had even considered it. Little Bear realized that the taste of his shame would have been much greater if he had failed that test, much greater than the pangs of hunger that he now felt.

Little Bear looked at the meat roasting by the fire and repositioned it to cook more evenly while thinking how good it smelled. The aroma of fresh venison roasting on a fire brought out his hunger in full. To ease the waiting, Little Bear tended his drying rack. Each piece of dried meat was inspected, the dried pieces being put into his satchel, the rest repositioned to help them dry evenly. This common chore that had to be done was completed without much effort or thought. For all the years that Little Bear could remember he always had some type of work to do; now he was beginning to see that the simple chores that he had done in his younger days were a needful part in keeping him alive today. Little Bear realized that his thinking was different, not seeing things as individual tasks but a series of actions that fit together like a dance, a dance of life. A deer would think of eating, drinking, looking for the next leaf to be eaten or the predator that wanted to eat it as individual events; Little Bear saw how the different parts of his life worked together to make a whole.

The sweet aroma of roasting meat was now overpowering, Little Bear could not resist. This morning's meal was a bit late coming after doing several chores, but this made it taste better. While eating this meal, the meat that was drying came to mind. Though dried deer meat did taste good, it would not be as savory as if it were freshly roasted, and would lose its appeal after eating it several days with no break. With that thought in mind, Little Bear looked at his fresh roasted meal and bit into it with a new relish.

The morning was passing as Little Bear finished his meal and put the roasting sticks aside. The sun shone into the little recess though partially being blocked by the deer hide. Clouds were slowly drifting by, larger ones following the smaller, and Little Bear could sense rain in the air. With the floor of the recess sloping slightly down away from the mountain, there was little chance of getting wet unless the winds shifted and came out of east which was not very likely. Looking around to make sure everything was under cover, Little Bear felt satisfied with the condition of his lakeside home. Turning back to read the sky, it was easily observed that the clouds were darkening and rain would soon be upon him.

Better to be careful and prepare for any long stay he thought. There was at least three days of firewood tucked into the little shelter, but now was the time to retrieve more in case his stay was to be longer. Also, he wanted to leave a good supply in return for the kindness that someone else had shown in leaving a well-stocked shelter. Little Bear began to question who that would have been, a member of his own tribe, the Yarric, or maybe someone from a completely different tribe. What would a Yarric think if he knew that it was Little Bear of the Kengeia tribe who used the wood they had so carefully stored away? This amused Little Bear and he gave a slight chuckle. "A Yarric provides wood for me," he laughed, "and now will I provide wood for a Yarric?" With a light heart and smile, Little Bear peered out of the recess, being a bit more cautious with the thought of the Yarric, and not seeing any sign of movement, quickly he emerged and went in search of wood.

Cautiously gathering several armfuls of fuel, never stripping any area clean and thereby betraying his presence, Little Bear diligently worked at this task unaware that eyes were watching him, and more than one pair.

CHAPTER 6 - WAITING UPON THE SPIRITS

A good week's supply of wood was found and neatly stacked in a way that would keep it dry and still allowed Little Bear a bit of space to move about. The drying meat was checked, a few pieces stowed away in his satchel, the rest repositioned for even drying. One piece was removed, closely inspected, and with a smile bit into. Slowly chewing, Little Bear turned, stepped out to the berm and looked out over the lake.

The Lake reflected the dark clouds above, now one large mass that blocked out the sun and draped the land in its cool shadow. A cold moist wind flowed down the mountainside with the promise of rain soon behind, the land was becoming quiet, the birds and animals were finding shelter, hoping to hide from the approaching rains. Little Bear swatted at a small swarm of mosquitoes that buzzed about his face that were hoping for a quick easy meal. The shelter was ready, provisions enough for a short stay lay at hand, now was the time to wait upon the Spirits. Was the darkening sky their approach, the cold wind the breath of the Spirits and not the storm? Little Bear wondered as uneasiness at being alone upon the mountainside started creeping in.

The cool wind started to bite as Little Bear sat cross legged upon the little berm in front of his camp. He had hoped the Spirits would quickly come, patience not a virtue of the young, and that hope was unfulfilled. Time dragged on as the clouds got darker and the entire scene in front of him seemed devoid of life. The mixture of fear of the unknown, the hard rock that he sat upon, and the wind that chilled was taking its toll upon him. Turning, his fire looked low but warm and inviting. Would the Spirits seek him out in the shelter or would they prefer this prominent position, perched on the mountainside awaiting their presence? Doubts about what to do flooded his mind as he wondered if he should have some sense of the proper way to await the Spirits' arrival.

Little Bear's muscles ached, the rock he sat upon seeming to be even harder than before, and his arms were covered with goose flesh as he shivered in the wind. Slowly, stiffly, he stood up and stretched, feeling like his joints had started turning to stone like the one on which he sat. It was hard to move as each step back into the shelter was painful and took a lot of effort to get his body to move. Little Bear tended the dying fire by adding wood then holding his cold hands over the little flame, the warmth felt good. Hours of sitting in the cold wind had sapped his strength, and it would not be wise to continue in this same fashion of waiting upon the Spirits. Little Bear took his buffalo skin and draped it over his shoulders and back, then standing on the fires edge, he leaned in close to the flames to gain as much heat as he could.

The flames were now dancing on the newly laid wood, radiating warmth in their merriment. The heat, as well as the buffalo skin, felt good, but Little Bear could not join in with the frolicking flames and their dance and this made him lonely. Looking around, the dark little recess with his few possessions, he felt lifeless except for the mosquitoes. Turning towards the opening of the recess, the wind was blowing hard causing the trees to sway to and fro. Occasional leaves and raindrops blew past making their way down the mountainside to the lake below. Casting his gaze up and seeing the clouds boil as they rolled by made Little Bear feel small and insignificant. The emptiness within grew like a hole in his stomach, the darkness of the storm now seemed magnified and Little Bear longed for the companionship of the tribe. The weight of the cold, the stiffness, and the loneliness became too much to bear and he sank down on his knees, and pulled the buffalo skin tightly around him. There was a pain from within that was crushing, sapping all strength, preventing him from even thinking, it just held Little Bear in its embrace with invisible hands and would not let him go.

Tears flowed. He hurt from a wound that could not be seen and it tore his insides. There was no time, no sense of where it had come from or of any way to ease its grip, only an all-encompassing pain that held him tight. Soft sobs were heard and Little Bear realized they were his. He focused on the sound that seemed so loud but in reality was only a whisper and he gained strength by hearing a voice, even if it was his own. Next the crackle of the fire was heard and Little Bear saw that the flames were still dancing, oblivious to his presence, his pains. He watched them dance. He had brought them to life, fed them, and was their only source of subsistence and they knew it not, they only danced to the crackling music they made. The spell was broken though Little Bear did not notice. The pain within was fading and he did not know it; the tears stopped from eyes that were entranced by the flames of a warm inviting fire.

Were they really alive? With a shaky hand Little Bear reached for another piece of wood and held it out to the flames, then watched them slowly dance upon it. Calmness now slowly returned to him. With each breath tension was exhaled and the flow of tears dried up. Now the patter of the rain was heard, coming in waves with driving gusts of wind that were blowing down the mountainside. The flames dancing upon the stick that he held were growing, crackling in a warm inviting song. Comforted by the fire which offered warmth and a soothing song. his loneliness abated. Little Bear gently set the flaming stick back in the fire and added more wood to enlarge and draw more comfort from it. Though not really hungry, a meal of fresh cooked meat also seemed to offer comfort on that lonely mountainside so three choice pieces were skewered with the cooking sticks and placed where they would slowly roast. With a little time to wait for the meat to roast, Little Bear wrapped his buffalo skin around him and laid down on his side facing the fire to watch the flames and his meal, blinked his eyes and was asleep.

Long Cloud had been watching for a while like a cat patiently waiting on its prey, not moving, hoping to be undetected. He knew that the best way to remain unseen was to be back in the dark shadows and not move. Without the benefit of the sun or movement it would be a cold days' watch and with the cold came stiffness. This was not good if a need arose that called for action, but there was no choice. Long Cloud did the best he could in finding comfortable cover that was sheltered from the wind. Now came the long watch.

Long Cloud waited and watched. He saw Little Bear cautiously arise and peer out over the shelf that was in front of the small recess. He saw him dispose of the deer carcass, clean up, gather wood, and go back into his small camp. Hours went by watching Little Bear sit on the berm waiting for the Spirits, and these were painful hours as Long Cloud's muscles stiffened up from the cold and lack of movement, and still he watched. Sometimes he scanned the mountainside for any movement, hoping not to see the Yarric, hoping not to see the rain coming down the mountainside, but always watching. He considered finding another hiding place where there was a better view, a little more covered from the wind. There were no large trees to hide in, and the ones that were about offered little cover. He must see but not be seen. To be above or on equal level with Little Bear and see into the recess of his camp would mean being much closer but that would make it harder not to be discovered. This position would have to do until night came, depending on moon and clouds.

As the sky became darker with the thickening cloud cover and the smell of rain was sensed in the air, Long Cloud knew he had to make new plans. There had been no sign of anyone else on the mountainside and little chance of any with the weather turning. To be caught out in a spring rain on a high mountainside with no warm camp nearby was an unnecessary risk to take. Little knowledge of how Little Bear was handling his rite was being gathered at this point. Long Cloud made the decision that he would go back to his supplies and find what shelter he could until the rains passed.

Slowly Long Cloud backed out of his hiding place, muscles sore, joints stiff, and kept out of sight of Little Bear, and made his way in search of his stores and shelter. Little did Long Cloud know but a pair of eyes saw him and they were not Little Bear's.

CHAPTER 7 - BROKEN HORN

Slowly coming up from the lower south side of the lake earlier that morning was Broken Horn of the Yarric tribe. Broken Horn had left his tribe's camp two days earlier and was enroute to the recess that Little Bear was now in, not knowing that it was already in use. Two nights before then when he had left his tribe all was quiet and the tribe was sitting around a central fire listening to Running Water tell the children stories of the birth of the world and all the animals. A fitting time for such tales as the land was awakening from the sleep of winter into the birth of spring.

The fire felt good on Broken Horn's old bones. A Yarric of many years, a warrior and hunter, Broken Horn now felt the weight of those years. Hunting was now hard as he had slowed down. As his body did not move as fast, most of the young men would leave him behind on hunts. His eyes did not see clearly and many arrows missed their mark. Most of his time was now spent with the young boys, preparing them to handle a knife and bow and not out in the open on the hunt. Broken Horn would look at the young lads and smile. He knew their fathers, grandfathers, and their fathers, and knew these were the lifeblood of the tribe's future. Sadness would overcome him as he saw the young men leaving camp, knowing he was not joining them as they set out on many an adventure under the open skies. Memories of running hard, heart pounding, lungs drawing in volumes of fresh air haunted him; sweet memories that he would experience no more.

Slowly standing up, stiff muscles and old wounds reminded him that youth was past and there was no turning back to those long-ago times. Broken Horn turned to let his backside warm, facing the western sky and thought how sad it was that like the sun setting so it was with his life. The stars were coming out over Spirit Mountain, the home of his ancestors. He pondered whether it was soon to be his home also. A warrior should have no fear, yet there were times when death seemed close and Broken Horn had fought to stay alive. What was life, he mused. Was there truly a death? Or is death just another step in life where he would go to live, in some far-off place with his ancestors?

A light gust of wind pressed against his face and frame. It was cold and caused a few shivers which made the old wounds hurt once more. Holding on to this life was painful. There was the joy of living, but at this moment, this thought was stopped with the hoots of an owl. Somewhere in the distance this bird called out. Broken Horn stared into the night trying to see where the sound had come from. The stars were bright and seemed to crown Spirit Mountain; there were no clouds in the sky which made it seem so vast with an uncountable number of stars. Then a dark form silently soared above the nearby trees; a silhouette of a bird against the night sky. Time seemed to have stopped until it hooted again, then alighted from the trees not far away, and shivers returned to Broken Horn's spine. Then he heard his name, softly, almost noiselessly, like the sound of an owl flying; he heard his name being called from out of the darkness. The owl could be seen flying not far away. It turned and with it was the sound of a voice that said, "Come," and it flew off towards Spirit Mountain.

Broken Horn stood there. He felt nothing: not the warmth of the flames, the chill of the night or the aches in his aged body. The crackling of the fire was now unheard as were the voices of those around him. All that he heard was the echo of the softly spoken word, his name being spoken by the owl. "The owl called my name," he whispered to himself.

There was no question, he must go. When your time had come, when you had survived childhood, times of hunger, times of war; when you survived life into old age, there came a time when you would survive no more. The Spirits would look across the land and see those who were old and worn out. Whether to thin the tribe of old, dead, and dried up wood or out of compassion for the pains of the old, no one knew. The owl was sent, a messenger of the Spirits and he would call your name. The last adventure was now to start, to walk into the wilds and then join your ancestors.

The children were taught this as if it were a great honor. The young did not think of it and the old feared it. Death was to come to all, this was known, but how one died mattered. There was honor to die on a hunt in support of the tribe, to die with your enemy's blood upon your knife blade was truly a great honor, but to walk out into the wilds, to die of starvation, exposure, or be torn by a wild animal was to die as an old dog, not a warrior of the tribe. Broken Horn stood there, drained of all hope, an emptiness opened up on his insides and he felt hollow and so totally defeated that he thought the light wind itself could crush him. Slowly he sat down, his head dropped to his chest, and too weak to cry, the tears just flowed down unhindered as life continued on all around him.

The night wore on, the stories ended, the children went to their tepees, and still Broken Horn sat though the tears had long since dried on his old weathered cheeks. Older members of the tribe also started back to their tepees, noticing Broken Horn but giving him no real thought; he was a fixture of the tribe, one of the old wise ones, maybe lost in deep thought so best left alone, and they did. Soon only a few were left, and as they began to arise and leave, Chief Two Feathers, who had noticed earlier how quiet and still Broken Horn was, came and stood beside him and looked out to Spirit Mountain.

"Broken Horn," he said softly as if not to startle him if he were asleep, "you are quiet this evening."

Slowly Broken Horn raised his head, his eyes unfocused but looking towards Spirit Mountain. Chief Two Feathers patiently waited to hear what Broken Horn had to say, his silence spoke of someone in deep thought.

"The owl called my name." His voice was weak, drained of all energy, a voice that spoke of despair.

Chief Two Feathers felt a twinge inside, his heart felt for, reached out to Broken Horn. His mind flashed back in time and in contrast to this warrior that was now broken in defeat. He remembered a strong vibrantly brave warrior that he had always looked up to. He remembered the last couple of raids they had made together, when Broken Horn had taken many chances and yet always succeeded. Looking down on this now old man, he realized that Broken Horn had acted in a seemingly rash way those last times in the hope of falling as a brave warrior in battle, to die with honor and not as a tired old man. Knowing what lay ahead Chief Two Feathers thought that even dying of sickness was better than what was to come.

Looking back to Spirit Mountain, seeing the stars above, Chief Two Feathers took a deep breath.

"You have lived a long life, Broken Horn, your strength has served you well. Be proud as you go to join our fathers after living an honorable life that has served the tribe."

These were hollow words and Chief Two Feathers knew it, but what could he say? Broken Horn was about to set out and meet his death like an old dog that was totally used up, a warrior and hunter who was going to become prey for wild animals or die from exposure to the elements.

"My strength," Broken Horn started to say, wanting to spit in disgust, but he paused instead.

He wished for the strength and skill that he was so proud of, that kept him alive in so many conflicts; these he wished had failed him many years ago. Anger started to grow within him as he felt forced to endure a disdainful death, a horrid reward for his long service to the tribe. Why couldn't the Spirits give him one last battle, a death in glory and honor? But he held the anger within, Chief Two Feathers had always been a good friend, yet what could he say, what else could he do but speak the words that had been taught in the tribe from ages past.

He started again. "My strength has given me a long life that I have given to the tribe. Tomorrow my friend, I will speak with words of encouragement to let the tribe know that I am taking a journey to Spirit Mountain, and then into the stars to join our ancestors."

The anger had passed, Broken Horn had resolved to accept his fate and serve the tribe once more by holding to the traditions of old. Relieved that such a hard situation was going to pass peacefully, Chief Two Feathers put his strong hand on Broken Horn's shoulder to offer comfort and let him know of his appreciation. Some things were better said without words and this was one of them.

"We will have a great feast in your honor, tell stories of great feats that you accomplished, we will make a legend of you to be told for ages to come."

A weary smile appeared on Broken Horn's face. "Not the death I was looking for," he said as the despair left. "Help me to my feet my friend. Tomorrow I will make my preparations and on the following morning I will head out with my head held high as if off to battle."

Chief Two Feathers gave a strong arm and felt Broken Horn's iron grip as he pulled himself up. A warrior of great merit he thought to himself, to face a hard death like this should earn him high honors among our fathers. Broken Horn slowly walked back to his tepee, head held high, resolute in his decision to face death and not flinch, but he hurt inside with a sharp pain, knowing he was not going to die a warrior's death.

Word was out the next morning about Broken Horn hearing the owl call his name. Chief Two Feathers had told the council to go out and make this a happy occasion, stressing that Broken Horn was going home to be with his ancestors. "We must make this a festive evening, a celebration of a warrior going on to his reward," Chief Two Feathers had said.

Festive was not the mood in Broken Horn's tepee as a battle raged in mastering his emotions, to control his appearance and not show the despair that was consuming him from within. He looked at his possessions that were laid out in readiness to give away, each with a memory that would be conveyed along with it. Is this the total of my life, he thought, this small collection of things? Again, a wave of despair swept over him, shouldn't there be something more, he thought, something that matters, that would be lasting? Broken Horn thought of his wife who had died many years before while carrying their first and only child. Both died that night so long ago. His desire for a wife died with her. He loved her too much and in the pain of her passing, Broken Horn swore never to remarry and suffer that pain again. With her died his legacy, a child that was never born, a child that would have grown and given his life meaning. What am I leaving, he thought. With me dies my line, no one to add to the tribe?

Turning, Broken Horn stepped out of his tepee and waited a moment for his eyes to adjust to the morning light. The tribe was alive with the news of his calling, smiles were everywhere and it seemed everyone was looking at him with awe and respect. There was more, their greetings were full of happiness, they felt great joy for him, almost envious. The contrast hit him hard and Broken Horn struggled to understand. He was to face a shameful hard death and the tribe was happy. Confused as he was, he decided to watch and see what he could learn, to try and understand their joy.

A small group of children ran by, about five or six summers old. They laughed and giggled as a little dog ran with them, licking their hands and faces when they slowed, cleaning sticky fingers and faces after their morning meal. Broken Horn soon found himself laughing with them, watching the delight of these innocent faces. As they scampered off Broken Horn felt his heart lightened; happy children meant a healthy tribe.

Walking towards the center of camp, Red Dawn came up to him holding a mat with hot bread, and with reverence, she offered it quickly to him. "You have blessed my family so much, providing much meat for us over the years. I wanted to be the first to give you something to eat this morning." Broken Horn, a bit surprised, thanked her while taking the mat from her hands. He remembered several times her husband being sick and unable to hunt, of bringing fresh game to them. He had not given it much thought at the time as he was just helping the tribe stay strong. He knew their need and did what needed to be done. It felt good now to know that they remembered and still appreciated his efforts.

"That is very kind of you Red Dawn, this smells very good as I am sure it is. I will go sit by the fire and enjoy this fine meal," he said now with a smile on his face. As Broken Horn thanked her, he noticed Red Dawn glancing quickly back over her shoulder, there he noticed two other women with mats of food looking disappointedly towards them.

That morning sitting by the fire, he was obliged to eat three more meals specially prepared for him and each with thanks for many things that he had done over the years. Slowly finishing the last meal, he thought it would now take quite a while to starve after eating all this food. Getting up was a little difficult with such a full stomach and it seemed like his belly was ready to split wide with the slightest movement. I better hide when it comes to the noon meal, he thought, I cannot take another round of kindness so soon after the first one.

Walking around the camp, Broken Horn noted the different looks on the faces that passed him. The young boys looked at him in awe and asked if he was afraid of meeting the Spirits. Their honesty and inquisitiveness made him laugh and tell a story or two to the children. When Broken Horn walked away, the boys felt honored to have such a brave warrior take time to talk to them. A new feeling was starting to take over, the calmness that comes when everything seems right, and it was lifting weight off his tired old shoulders.

Older members of the tribe would look and seemed to take courage on seeing his calmness, knowing that they too would soon follow. Broken Horn could see the eyes of those he grew up with looking admiringly at him, their heads now held high as they drew strength in seeing a warrior without fear about to start a journey that they were to follow. Maybe, they thought, the last journey would not be so bad after all, and Broken Horn walked on with a new perspective that was forming with every face he came across.

The young men saw a warrior ready to go on his last quest with no sign of fear. They saw a brave move about camp as if it was any other day and they marveled. Being young they dreamed of adventures that could lead to honor, but also the possibility of injury or death, and that thought scared them. Now before them stood one who was about to walk up and meet his own death, how could he be so calm they wondered. Broken Horn watched them through the corner of his eye as they stepped back in hushed awe and then heard their muffled words of astonishment as he walked past them, bragging that they too would be brave like him. After years of seeing himself in a diminished view, he felt proud once more upon seeing the respect that he received. Stopping at his tepee and looking back over the tribe he sensed something new, a new sense of life, a sense that the tribe felt they were special and had an ideal to live up to. Broken Horn smiled, maybe, he thought, I am not an old dog hobbling off to die, not a useless old man at the end of his life. Maybe I have been given a gift that in my passing I will be making my tribe stronger. With that thought Broken Horn went into his tepee a different man than the one he was when he stepped out a few hours before.

Night came and there was an excitement about the main fire as everyone waited to hear Chief Two Feathers speak of Broken Horn. The moon slowly rose and an intense anticipation rose with it. The drums slowly started to beat, all eyes shot to the Chief's tepee, its flap parted and instantly it was quiet. Chief Two Feathers stepped out in his full battle array and stood up straight and strong. Holding the flap open as a sign of honor, Broken Horn came out equally dressed as if for battle to the sound of gasps from about the central fire. They walked together like two warriors ready to challenge an opposing force with a confidence in every step that would put fear in even a stout-hearted enemy. They walked up to the fire and stopped at the spot where the Chief usually sat. Council members were sitting flanked on either side allowing plenty of room for Chief Two Feathers and Broken Horn. Only the crackling of the fire could now be heard as all stared at the spectacle of the two warriors standing before them. The tribe valued strength and courage, a warrior's heart. Now two fine examples stood there, the flames of the fire sending a red light that accented their fierceness.

Chief Two Feathers raised his powerful arms high, his head leaned back and he belted out a warrior's cry as if challenging the sky itself. His voice reverberated through the entire tribe stirring up a passion deep within each person's heart and soul. Before his cry died down the council leapt to their feet and together let loose a singular cry, yet this cry also had the sound of joy like that of warriors heading off into battle. The overwhelming display of exuberance ignited an excitement in the tribe that could not be contained and soon everyone was on their feet dancing as the drums began again to beat which sounded like thunder rolling down the hills on a hot summer night. Broken Horn stood there taking in the scene, feeling the power of the drums and war cries vibration through his body. This is in honor of me, he thought, the tribe is sending me off on my last quest. They view me not as an old man but a warrior who has triumphed in life and is now setting off in search of a new conquest.

He was seeing his life in a new light. The warrior within was awaking once again, being fed by the excitement of the tribe. He looked at the tribe, his tribe that he had fought and provided for his whole life, and now they were giving him their energy. His muscles were old but not weak, and their strength was being rekindled, the very fabric of his being was feeling young again. Broken Horn started breathing deeper as he started swaying to the dance before him, the beat of the drums flowed through him. His arms rose high on their own and he let loose with a mighty roar and he was carried off into the dance.

It took a while for the tribe to vent their energy as the expectations of this evening had been growing throughout the day. Chief Two Feathers knew how to read his tribe and as the first members were beginning to tire, he signaled the drummers to slow down the tempo and then to stop when most of the tribe resumed their positions around the fire. It took only a few moments for those still dancing to notice and they too returned to their places about the fire. Chief Two Feathers alone stood, surveying the tribe and gauged that they had relieved enough energy to aid them in hearing his words, yet not so much as to hinder the excitement and dance when the drums were to start again. Satisfied, he spread out his arms and started.

"My people, it is a glorious night that we are in; a night to honor a great warrior who has lived among us."

Many yells of agreement rang out from around the fire which Broken Horn took in like food to his soul. Chief Two Feathers smiled as he stood there seeing his friend honored and at the same time his tribe binding together with the traditions of old. The truth of this tradition of the owl calling your name was a hard one to bear. They knew what the person being called was about to endure, but traditions were that which held the tribe together. Chief Two Feathers raised his arms again and there was quiet.

"My people," he started again, "Broken Horn is my friend. For many a summer we have hunted together, fought together, and gone on quests together. He has shared his strong arm, his wisdom, and life with the tribe. How many of you have received help from Broken Horn, benefited from the game he has caught or slept safely as he stood guard over the tribe? He has been an example of who we are and a leader in showing who we are to be."

Again, the tribe spoke up in a clamor of agreement, both young and old letting their voices be heard in a deafening roar. Broken Horn, though humbled, felt a combination of pride and satisfaction as he realized his many deeds were not long forgotten like the strength of his youth. All the days of dismay as limitations of age crept in were now being washed away in wave after wave of cheers that erupted over and over as Chief Two Feathers went on to relate many of his exploits.

It was now late into the evening after Chief Two Feathers and the council had finished relating many tales of Broken Horn and how his feats were equal to famous warriors of the past. Dancing had broken out on several occasions and was hard to contain as the excitement of the evening kept reaching new heights. Finally Broken Horn stood up looking like a vision of every proud warrior of the past rolled into one. The fire was lower now and the red glow of the coals illuminated every feature of this warrior in full battle dress with the shadows accenting his weather worn face that gave everyone the impression that this was not flesh and blood standing before them but an apparition of a warrior of old. A hush now came over the tribe as Broken Horn stood there looking proud and strong gazing over them. They watched his eyes slowly go from one end of the tribe to the other, seemingly looking at each of them with eyes that showed approval. Spreading his arms out wide, taking a deep breath and shifting his gaze to a place just over the fire, he began.

"My family, I am well pleased to call you my family." A slight murmur was heard as many felt a sense of pride in being considered a family member to such a mighty warrior of renown. "Since the death of my wife I have had but one family, the tribe. Everyone here is part of my family and I am proud of you as any father is proud of his child." A roar of approval and expressions of delight echoed all around the fire as the tribe was feeling honored by such a valued member of their tribe. Broken Horn stood there looking almost like a spirit himself in the glow of the fire with stars shining over his head, and everyone felt as if he was speaking to them individually.

"My family," he began again, "as you all know, the owl has called my name; the Spirits have sent their messenger for me to come to them and join our ancestors. This last quest that I am to go on I do with a glad heart in that I am to see all those that have gone on before us, yet with a sad heart in that we will be separated for a little while." No longer thinking of what he was soon to endure, partially caught up in the excitement of the evening and partially carrying on with his plan to strengthen the tribe in being a positive model in what he must do next, the integrity of the man who had lived his life for the tribe was shining through. "I will not make this evening any longer than it needs to be, the night is getting on. I have this one last thing to add as I am to be off on the morrow. If anyone has a message to give to one of your ancestors, a family member who has gone ahead of us, give it to me and I will tell it to them when I arrive in our new home in the stars."

With that Broken Horn sat down having said enough and hoping that he said nothing amiss. Again, the younger members jumped up to their feet and started the final dance of the night. Chief Two Feathers who was standing next to Broken Horn reached over and put his hand on his shoulder. "Well said Broken Horn, your words have strengthened the tribe. I am proud to be your friend." There was no time to say anything else as people started coming up to them. Many of the tribe, especially the elder members, came with relief in their eyes as if a heavy weight had been lifted from them, the fear of what awaited now seemed easier to bear and they wanted to thank and say goodbye to Broken Horn.

CHAPTER 8 - WHEN TRIBES COME TOGETHER

Now Broken Horn was quietly watching as Long Cloud backed out of his position and circled wide, disappearing further up the mountainside. Looking above the lake where he knew this little recess lay, the faint glow of a fire could be discerned. There were several possibilities for a brave spying on someone who had made camp but here on Spirit Mountain it seemed pretty clear, this brave was acting as guardian for whoever was up there.

The wind was picking up and it had the smell of rain which would make for a miserable night out in the open. Looking back towards where he had last seen Long Cloud there was no trace of his passing. Evening was approaching and it would soon be too dark for making a treacherous climb on the mountainside. A decision was made, Broken Horn slowly moved out from where he was standing and carefully made his way around the opposite side of the lake from which Long Cloud had been last seen and headed towards the recess. There was little for Broken Horn to fear, his death was soon to be so no matter what was to occur it would not matter. Still, it would be best for his arrival at the recess to be a surprise to whoever was there and not the other way around.

It took a while for Broken Horn to make the trip, slowed by both his caution and a body that was not as nimble as it had once been. Coming in from the south side, Broken Horn peered around the rocks to see what awaited him. It was now fully dark, only a faint glow from the moon behind the clouds that coated the night sky. Little Bear's small fire put out a light that was easily seen even with the deerskin that was hung to partially obscure it. There sat Little Bear with his back to the rock wall and the fire before him. His head hung down upon his chest and he was breathing softly in his slumber. Scanning the recess, he saw Little Bear's bow carefully laid aside, his stores, the supply of wood, everything in neat order. Gauging what he saw, Broken Horn was sure Little Bear was alone and he breathed a sigh of relief as this was going to be a bit easier than he had first thought. Looking back at Little Bear, he estimated his age at being between 14 and 16 summers old and rightly assumed this was his rite of manhood. But an odd one he thought for his clothing showed that his tribe was obviously from the south therefore there must be something special concerning this boy who would soon be a man.

A sizzle was heard and Broken Horn's keen eye spied a few pieces of fresh meat on skewers near the fire, the boy must have nodded off waiting for his evening meal to cook. Broken Horn smiled and looked back to Little Bear, life seemed precious now that his was so near to an end and the sight of this scene spoke of fresh life and touched this old man's heart. True he was not of the same tribe but he seemed like a child from Broken Horn's point of view and all children were precious.

A final decision now had to be made, to stay and get shelter for the night from the coming storm or retreat and spend the night in the elements. If he left his death would come sooner from exposure, not something to look forward to. If he stayed, providing he could manage Little Bear, it meant a relatively comfortable night. Two days by himself was tiring and a little company would be welcomed, also looking at this young lad reminded Broken Horn how much he enjoyed listening to the young, fresh with the life that was youth. Taking a final view of the recess, noting especially the bow was placed with care near the wood and the knife strapped to Little Bear's hip, Broken Horn carefully crept in. Like a cougar stalking his prey, he was slow and silent not making the slightest sound. With great care he sat down next to the fire laying the little bundle of supplies behind him; Little Bear slept on.

When Little Bear awoke, he would be startled and in that moment would be danger. Broken Horn was not afraid, he felt he could handle any reaction unless Little Bear jumped back and grabbed his bow. The best course of action seemed to be just to remain calm, be still, and wait. Getting comfortable, sitting cross legged with upturned hands on his knees, eyes half open looking ahead, Broken Horn quietly started singing the story of creation in what he thought was Little Bear's tongue. He started so softly that it could barely be heard. Slowly getting louder until he was sure Little Bear could make out the words when he awoke, Broken Horn sang on as the rains started to fall.

A dream came to Little Bear; a voice out of nowhere could be heard while he was standing on the ledge overlooking the little lake. He could see stars shining brightly overhead that seemed closer than they ever had been before. The lake shone brightly with silver ripples that looked like the silver lochs on an old man's head flowing over his shoulders. "Listen, listen carefully and you will be led in times of need," the voice said, coming from nowhere, yet being everywhere.

The stars in Little Bear's vision pulsated brightly in the sky and could be seen reflected on the lake amid the silver ripples. Now all the trees and surrounding mountainside were outlined in silver which gave them the impression of being very old, aged and wise.

"Listen, listen for wisdom, for it shall come from many sources," the voice spoke again.

Little Bear felt no fear but only wondered at where the voice was coming from. Looking about him, he now saw animals and people of many tribes walking about, all glowing in the silver light. They were moving about, unaware of each other as they passed within an arm's length of one another. They held their heads high, proud, full of confidence, with an air that spoke to their having a secret knowledge or wisdom. Little Bear marveled at the vision before him, his full attention focused on the scene as it unfolded.

"Listen, listen and learn," the voice spoke again. "When there is need, we will speak, when there is choice we will guide, when there is danger, we will provide." With these words the silver scene faded slowly and a slight chill was felt in the calm of its passing.

As day darkens to night, the night now had darkened to blackness as the clouds thickened and only a hint of a red glow from the fire was sensed through his closed eyes. Rain and wind could now be heard along with the crackle of a small fire, Little Bear realized that he was dozing beside his fire. In the wind was a quiet deep voice that slowly grew until he could make out the words. Softly the voice continued, now steadily droning on, telling a tale, a story that he had heard before, the story of the birth of the world and the creation of all that was in it. He had heard the story many times by the fire in camp, sitting with his friends as the old ones sung this and many other tales. The song was comforting, its familiar words like the presence of a good friend on a lonely night and thinking this was part of a dream he just sat there listening to it go on.

"Ka-boom," thunder roared as a torrent of rain pelted the mountainside. The lightning shown bright through Little Bear's closed eyes as he stiffened and fell back a bit, stopping his fall with his arms quickly thrown back against the recessed mountain side. His eyes opened wide but were slow in adjusting to the dim light of the dwindling fire. All thoughts were gone, his senses instantly on edge striving to grasp his surroundings. The wind and rain wildly racing down the mountainside made Little Bear feel hemmed in, the crackle of a dying fire offered some warm assurance, and the familiar song in an aged voice was a comfort, but only for a moment as his mind grasped the reality that he was not dreaming and the voice shouldn't be there!

Broken Horn, a warrior of many summers, was not easily startled and always ready for the unexpected. As the rains turned into a storm, he knew there was a good chance that the thunder would come. He knew that with its loud voice the young lad that he was watching would wake in a start and controlling the moment would make the difference between a peaceful night and an unwanted fight, or possibly an unwanted death.

The song continued in Broken Horn's steady low voice, his eyes still half open staring ahead, past Little Bear, while his turned-up hands on crossed knees stayed motionless. Though ready to strike, to move quickly to defend from a blow, he gave no indication of any threat, of any movement. Every second that passed was a step from rash action on the lad's part, and if he played things right, the better chance for a peaceful outcome.

Little Bear froze, he could tell where the voice was coming from, his eyes adjusting to the low light, he could now make out the form of Broken Horn. Where moments before there was no fear with his vision and the surreal nature of what he had been seeing, now fully awake he knew that there was real danger about and he had to respond or he could die. In a flash Little Bear leaped back on his feet, his hand seized the knife that was strapped to his hip and held it low, ready to strike or defend. His eyes strained first at Broken Horn and then quickly around the little recess. Seeing no one else his eyes quickly focused on the one sitting by his little fire who had not moved a muscle.

Broken Horn just sat there, softly singing his song of creation, seemingly unconcerned or unaware of Little Bear's presence. But Broken Horn was highly aware, though not looking directly at this youth, he saw his every move, was reading every sign to know what he might do. Broken Horn was ready to spring into action at the first hint of danger. His song continued, each word would sow thoughts of doubt into this young man, doubts of danger and hopefully seed his mind with an overpowering curiosity.

Little Bear slowly edged to one side to bring the small fire between them and his back to the opening between the rock wall and the deerskin that was stretched out over the mouth of the recess. Staring intently, he saw the strong arms of a warrior with upturned hands. He eased a little, seeing that he was not under attack at the moment. The dress of this uninvited apparition was not familiar, but Little Bear had met few from other tribes and those were from the plains in the south that also followed the buffalo. He now looked to the face, well-worn with deep lines that were accented by the glow of the dying fire, and then there was the hair, locks of silver that reflected red in the dim light.

As Little Bear stared, sizing up this motionless invader of his space, he now heard the song that was being sung and it brought puzzlement that showed on his face. He had heard that song before, he knew it from his childhood, his eyes widened, he had heard it in the vision that he had just had. The tension in his arms eased as he brought the knife a little closer to his side and he stood up a little straighter. Broken Horn still did not move though he saw all and knew things were going well. Little Bear looked back upon the silver mane that was glowing in the fire light and remembered his vision. Were the vision and what he was now seeing one?

"Who are you?" Little Bear blurted out in a voice of challenge but a tone of someone grasping to understand.

Broken Horn continued his song, it was important not to respond as one responded to equals. The tribes to the south were not that aggressive, but this youth might attack like a cornered animal or feel he has to prove his manhood in battle. If this were a rite of manhood, he would be questioning how a warrior should respond to the meeting of another warrior, but his first reaction hinted of something more than a meeting of a man. If he were on a spirit quest, he would be questioning if what was sitting before him was flesh and blood. If that was the case, it would be best to keep him guessing for as long as possible.

Little Bear was feeling a tingling running up his spine and he did not know what to do. Was this a wandering warrior of the Yarric, someone to fear or was this one of the Spirits that sat before him, and why was he singing the song of creation, the song he had just heard in his vision? If he was Yarric he must

91

show no fear, if spirit he must show respect and show that he was ready to become a man. Still holding his knife ready, Little Bear slowly stood erect, pushing his chest out and holding his head high.

"I am Little Bear, warrior of the Kengeia. Who are you who have come to my fire?" He tried to speak in a commanding tone, showing no fear.

Broken Horn laughed to himself, I have him now, and the danger is now past. He knew the tribe and with his name he could control the moment. This youth is trying to impress me, a warrior at his age, he thought and it took a lot of control not to laugh out loud. Pausing his song, Broken Horn let the silence work on Little Bear's imagination as it would keep him off guard and further the impression that he was not in control.

The wind was raging outside, only occasional gusts reached within the recess to disturb the flames of the dying fire. The tension of the encounter was magnified by sounds of the storm, yet Little Bear only heard silence when the singing had stopped. Now in the voice of a Chief speaking to a child came Broken Horn's response.

"Is this the welcome of the Kengeia, a dying fire and no offer of the meat that is roasting upon it?"

Little Bear was stunned and taken off guard again. He was expecting an answer, hoping to know who or what was before him, but to be kindly rebuked like a child made the situation seem unreal and gave him no answer. He had heard age in the voice, strength and confidence, yet also a fatherly tone. Most of his fear was now replaced by curiosity, no danger was felt in the air, but he still needed to know who he faced. Perplexed, not willing to leave his question unanswered, Little Bear spoke again, this time in a humbler tone.

"Who is it that I share my fire with?"

Broken Horn had won, the tension was broken and Little Bear dropped the challenge from his voice and stance. Still, it was best to keep him off balance, to answer his question in such a way as to keep him guessing. Without moving, without changing the focus of his half open eyes, Broken Horn now spoke in a deep tone that seemed as if he were declaring his existence to the world, and yet to no one at the same time.

"I have given life to some and death to others; I am the giver of life and death. I have walked the earth and have seen many born, live life, and die; I am old in the age of men. I have listened to the cooing of the mourning dove, the cawing of the crow in the noon sun, the hooting of the owl at night; I am the keeper of wisdom."

Little Bear stiffened at the words of 'listened' and 'wisdom' and this did not escape the notice of Broken Horn.

"I have watched endless mornings come to life in the rising sun, days die in a blood-stained sky, nights shimmer in the silver light of the stars; I am the watcher of the ages."

Again, a shiver went up Little Bear's spine as Broken Horn spoke of a "silver light' and he stepped back. Broken Horn saw this and realized that there was something in his words that startled this youth. He paused to consider. Little Bear had reacted to two things that he had said, two things that had triggered a memory. It was not physical fear, he thought, so it must be related to a word given in his preparation or to a vision he had had. Thinking quickly that Little Bear was supposed to have received some vision on Spirit Mountain, Broken Horn took a chance.

"Sit and tell me of the vision," Broken Horn said in his calm deep voice.

Little Bear was stunned, more than ever it seemed this was a Spirit, and he knew of his vision? Yet he looked as if he was of flesh and blood, how could that be? Fear started to seep in, alone with a Spirit, he took a step back.

Broken Horn watched as a new challenge emerged, his intention was not to scare and not drive him out into the cold night. He was quickly growing fond of this youth, not seeing an enemy, only a youth who was starting his life, and life seemed so much more precious now. Also seen in Little Bear were so many of the youth of his own tribe with their airs and ambitions,

Broken Horn could not help but to feel the need to assist Little Bear in his quest of manhood, and for that he needed him to stay in the recess while the storm raged outside.

"The fire needs more wood and the meat is ready to be eaten," Broken Horn said now in the soft tone of a grandfather. "Are you not going to offer me the comfort of your fire and to share your evening meal?"

Little Bear stood still trying to make sense of all of this. He felt a cold wet wind occasionally on his back and the thought of running out into the night did not sound like a good choice, and then this is what he came here for, to hear from the Spirits. If he were to run, how could he face the tribe, Black Eagle, Rolling Thunder, Long Cloud, or his mother? No matter what happened, he had to stay.

Now came the question, do the Spirits eat? Many were the stories of Spirits taking the form of man or animal and they did eat. Little Bear, noticing his knife was the still held in his hand, slowly put it back in its sheath. Without taking an eye off his guest, he reached over, picked up several pieces of wood and carefully put them on the fire. Then he slowly picked up a skewer of meat that had the biggest piece on it and placed it in easy reach of Broken Horn, then sat on the opposite side of the fire.

Broken Horn now felt good. He would be warm and dry tonight, enjoy a meal of fresh meat prepared for him, and not have a fight. He had not driven Little Bear out into the night, and he was to have company one last time. Little Bear tensed up as Broken Horn slowly reached over to pick up the skewer of meat.

"Thank you, Little Bear, warrior of the Kengeia, I shall remember this gift that you have freely given me this night," Broken Horn said in a warm voice.

Little Bear eased up as Broken Horn's hand slowly moved back and held the skewer over his lap. Little Bear did not feel that the gift was freely given as there was no way he could refuse the request. Being called a "warrior of Kengeia" felt good but he was not sure this was being said in truth or jest.

"What shall I call you?" Little Bear asked, a tremble in his voice.

Broken Horn had accomplished what he wanted and more. He had controlled the situation and it could now be seen in Little Bear's eyes and voice that he did not know if he was seeing a man or a spirit. For the time being, Broken Horn felt it was best to keep him guessing.

"I am known by many names in many tongues by many different people," he said in a matter-of-fact way. Pausing just a moment, he then looked directly at Little Bear for the first time, switched to a warmer fatherly tone, "You can call me Broken Horn. With that said Broken Horn raised the skewer up and took a bite of roasted meat.

"You have done well Little Bear, to come this far, prepare this camp, and get this deer that you have cooked and given me." Broken Horn took another bite and slowly chewed it waiting for some response from Little Bear. The exact nature of Little Bear's quest was still unknown, and more hints were needed to maintain the ambiguity. Knowing that youth was never patient, it would not take long before the first question arose.

Little Bear sat there. To face the unknown brought on fear; to see the unknown sitting across the fire was terrifying. It took all the courage and willpower that Little Bear had not to run out into the night. He had not mastered his fear, he had only not let it control him. Little Bear was afraid to move, afraid to stay; all of his attention was on this apparition sitting across the fire slowly eating a piece of his evening meal.

"Little Bear," Broken Horn said in a warm tone. Little Bear cringed as even such a fatherly voice was frightening, "eat some meat before it burns, it would be wrong to waste it after the deer gave its life that you may live".

The words were a puzzle. These were rare things to happen: the rite of manhood and to see a spirit in human form. To show concern over a piece of meat as his mother had many times before did not seem to fit. Also, he noticed Broken Horn had said the deer had given its life for him. He did not include himself which would suggest that as a spirit he did not need food. There was no time to consider these things further as Little Bear did not want Broken Horn to become angry by his not doing as he was told. Keeping an eye on him, Little Bear slowly reached over to the nearest of the two skewers left on the fire and pulled it back, then slowly started eating. He noticed no flavor or texture; he was hardly aware of what he was doing. His attention was on the one sitting on the other side of the fire who was slowly eating the meat that he had prepared.

Broken Horn could see the tension, the fear in Little Bear. Getting him to eat, to do this mundane task would have a calming effect as it focused his attention on several different points which would give fear less opportunity to take hold of him.

"All life is sacred," Broken Horn started saying, now holding up his skewer before him, rolling it back and forth, while looking intently at the freshly cooked meat upon it. "When life is taken it must not be wasted. Life should support life, and this deer has given its life to support yours." Broken Horn paused, deep in thought. He knew his life was soon to come to an end just as the deer's had. A somber look came to his face and Little Bear took this to be the seriousness of his words.

"Do not waste life Little Bear," he said slowly, "all life has value. Take it if you must, feed your family, protect your tribe, but do not take the gift of life unless you have to."

Broken Horn paused, took a deep breath, and took another bite from his skewer. Little Bear watched him as his eyes glazed over in thought, slowly chewing. Fear had slowly ebbed away and what he saw was a grandfather talking to his grandson, trying to relate wisdom while he still could. Wasn't this who the Spirits were, caretakers of the tribes, father of them all?

They sat in silence finishing their skewers. A warm calmness rolled over Little Bear though he was still a bit nervous. Picking up the last skewer he offered it to Broken Horn.

"No my son, you have worked hard and need your strength, I have no need of it."

Little Bear wondered at this. If he had no need of food, why then did he eat the first skewer? This was of little concern though. What was important was what did Broken Horn have to say to him? He started eating the last skewer, not knowing what else to say. Broken Horn was a little uneasy with the quiet, all of the events up to that point were to his liking but to continue on he needed to know more details of Little Bear's quest. It was important to control their conversation, to keep it focused on Little Bear. Little Bear had not started relating his vision and Broken Horn had to be wary since if he were a spirit, he should know of the vision and not have to ask what it was, but then a thought came to mind. If on a quest you were to learn from the Spirits, then he would help Little Bear learn.

"Visions are a gift of the Spirits," Broken Horn started, now looking into Little Bear's eyes in a kind manner, speaking with the warm voice of a father wanting to instruct his child. "Sometimes to teach, sometimes to warn. Listen well and you will be led in times of peace and times of peril."

Little Bear was unsure of himself. A spirit had come to talk to him, was kind and gentle, but he felt fear. Scared though he was, he knew he must master his fear and remember to bring back all that was said to the council on his return. With his empty skewer in his hands, Little Bear looked back into the dark eyes that were framed by a weather-worn face that glowed red in the fire light.

"You must be able to read the signs and visions that you are given Little Bear," he continued, "to understand what is shown will help you and your tribe. Each vision has its purpose; it may show one thing or it may show many. Some will be for the moment, others will not occur for many summers to come."

Broken Horn, though his eyes were still looking towards Little Bear, they were not focused for he was now seeing the many visions that he had seen in the past. There was silence for a moment as Broken Horn considered, looking for a common thread, a way to help Little Bear see.

Little Bear was attentive now, interested in what was being

said, especially since he had questions about his own vision. A combination of curiosity and the impertinence of youth could no longer be contained.

"Why do the Spirits speak through visions and dreams and not words that are easy to understand?"

Little Bear let out this question without thinking, his curiosity being greater than his fear.

Broken Horn came back from his thoughts. This was good. The dangers were gone. They were both safe and warm by the fire as the storm blew by outside the little haven on the mountainside, and now the evening would be filled with conversation as long as he kept control of the moment. To keep one step ahead of this youth should not be hard. It would be a game of wits.

"The ways of the Spirits are not the ways of men, Little Bear," he said with a smile. "Be content that men are given the benefit of the Spirits' wisdom. Now is the time to learn how well you can see that wisdom."

Again, Broken Horn had to take a chance to keep the illusion going and for that, he needed to know more of Little Bear's quest. For him to be sent so far on his rite was unusual, some sign must have been given to have allowed such a thing to happen. Now was the time to be direct and master the situation.

"Tell of the visions that were seen, the signs and how they were read so that you were brought here. Tell me of the vision you have seen and how you read it. From there we will discuss their meaning and I will strengthen your insight, helping you to see how to read visions and signs."

"But why not tell me what my vision means, and then I would know how to read it?" Little Bear asked, wondering why he needed to repeat what was already known.

"How is one taught to shoot a bow?" Broken Horn replied. "The youth is first given a bow and is allowed to get the feel of it, to hold it, to shoot arrows as he feels fit. Too often the youth thinks it is easy and says he knows how to shoot and will not listen to instruction. Only after his attempt on his own when his

98

arrows go amiss, will he then be shown how to stand right. Then with his stance corrected, he is shown how to aim. When his arrow goes closer to the target, will he continue to listen. This way the youth takes what knowledge he has and changes for the better. Let us find out how well you read the signs and then I will help you see more clearly."

Little Bear thought for a moment, if he could not see the meaning of the vision. What would Broken Horn think of him? That he was too young to have started the rite? He was afraid of being embarrassed by not knowing how to read the vision. But what could he do? He could not argue with a spirit. Lowering his head so as not to look into his eyes. Little Bear started from the beginning, telling of Black Eagle and how he read the signs that started his quest. He told of his travels to Spirit Mountain hoping to impress Broken Horn with his swift pace and the shooting of the grouse and deer, the setting up of his camp. Then came the hard part as he did not know what the vision meant, yet he did have to say something. Taking a deep breath, he told of the vision, the voice saying "Listen," the silver shining stars, the trees, people, and animals. Little Bear became quiet, thinking intently what this meant, all the while hoping that Broken Horn would now explain their meaning.

Broken Horn had visions in the past and he pondered what the Spirits were trying to tell Little Bear. He considered Black Eagle's reading of the sign, though he did not see this himself, he trusted Black Eagle's wisdom. Their tribes had interacted on occasion, both in trade and battle, from that limited contact he knew a little of Black Eagle, Rolling Thunder, and a few of the council and knew that there was wisdom in their ranks. Black Eagle had seen in the sign that the Spirits had singled out Little Bear. They had a purpose, plans for his life. Broken Horn understood that the will of the Spirits was more important than the individual, more important than the tribe, and it was to be followed no matter what. Since the Spirits had called Little Bear and then given him a vision, it was best to aid Little Bear in understanding what he was shown. Looking at him, Broken

Horn did not see an adversary, he saw a youth and that spoke of life and it touched his heart.

Little Bear was now quiet after relating his vision, waiting for an interpretation. Broken Horn smiled, he felt he knew what the vision meant but wanted Little Bear to start thinking, to take the first step in reading visions and not to depend on others.

"You did well in relating your vision Little Bear," he said warmly, giving the impression of a grandfather talking to his grandson again. "Now tell me, how do you read what you have seen?"

This was not what Little Bear wanted to hear and it felt like a pit was now in his stomach and growing. He felt that he was being forced to give an answer and to interpret his vision and there was no way out. Taking a deep breath in resignation of what he must do, Little Bear, looking into the fire, used a stick and shifted the coals and considered what he had seen.

"I was told to listen," Little Bear started, not knowing what to say but hoping that he might stumble on the meaning, "this was repeated three times because it is important to listen and know the will of the Spirits."

"That is good Little Bear," Broken Horn responded, seeing him struggle and knowing the need for encouragement, "you will gain much if you listen carefully to that which is given to you. The Spirits will teach you, give you wisdom, and lead you in times of need to help you, your tribe, and other tribes so do not waste the gift of wisdom and direction that they give. Now what else do you see?"

Little Bear relaxed, feeling that he was on the right track and also feeling the warm tone of Broken Horn's words, he continued.

"The stars and trees, the people and animals, they all glowed which means that they are all alive."

He said this rather cautiously, it was known that all these had Spirits within and that they all lived. Little Bear hoped this would be accepted as an answer and that Broken Horn would add meaning to it.

Broken Horn smiled again knowing what Little Bear was doing. Reading signs could be hard depending on what was meant to be said by the Spirits. This vision did not seem that hard but Little Bear would naturally feel overwhelmed by all that was happening. Knowing it was best not to press him too much, Broken Horn relieved Little Bear's fears.

"You are right Little Bear, for all these things are alive and have Spirits. Know also there is much wisdom to be learned from all of them. The Spirits will speak not just through visions and signs but also through the stars and trees, rocks and water, people and animals. Listen well and you will gain wisdom through all of them."

"Know this also Little Bear; you have been called out of your tribe for a special purpose. Right now, you are coming into manhood, becoming a brave member of the Kengeia tribe. The path that is laid before you is not because you are special, so do not think because you were chosen that you are better than others of your tribe. The choices of the Spirits are not due to the merits of those they choose. You must work hard to prepare yourself so that you will not only be a brave of your tribe, but ready for when you are called upon by the Spirits. In times to come, you will have tasks to perform that will require your strength and courage, but to succeed you will need to listen for wisdom, need to read the signs, and to act honorably. This is a simple message but important for you and your tribe, remember well."

"On your return Black Eagle will help you in learning how to read visions and signs. Spend time with your council, and learn all you can from them so that in times of need you will be ready to act quickly with courage and wisdom."

As Broken Horn continued to speak with encouragement and direction, using the names of the council that Little Bear had not mentioned, all doubt that he was not a spirit now had passed. Little Bear had gone from being scared, taking all his willpower to keep from fleeing, to feeling like a child in the presence of an elder, to being humbled in the presence of a spirit. Broken Horn had helped set Little Bear in the belief that he was not special even though he was being called upon by the Spirits, this was a belief he would never stray from. This was also important for the other tribes as a brave who was not ruled by honor but thinking themself special and above the customs of the tribes was a danger to all.

The main brunt of the storm had passed, night wore on and only a light rain was now heard without. It was late and Broken Horn was feeling tired and knew he needed a little sleep. He had taken a lot of time reading the vision and expounding on virtue and courage, hoping to develop, in the short time he had, the desire to be honorable. The Kengeia tribe was not a threat to his own tribe so aiding Little Bear would not hurt but might in fact be a benefit as a nearby tribe of honor could be helpful in time of need.

"Little Bear," Broken Horn now spoke after a long pause, "you need some sleep before morning arrives. Put some more wood on the fire to keep yourself warm and then get some rest. Tomorrow you need to restock the wood supply for those who will use this shelter in the future and then you must be off to your tribe."

Though Little Bear had questions to ask, he did not have the courage to press Broken Horn so with reluctance, he added wood to the fire, laid down with his buffalo skin pulled tightly around himself and slowly drifted off to sleep.

Broken Horn sat as comfortably as he could, feeling it was best to get a little sleep in a sitting position with the intent to move on in the morning before Little Bear awoke and before the brave that he had seen watching from below the lake returned. If all went well, he could be off, circling around for most the day and returning to the shelter before nightfall with Little Bear on his way back to his tribe. By the time the sky was showing a little color and the stars were fading, Broken Horn carefully fed the fire and looked at Little Bear in its low light. A smooth faced youth was all he saw and, in his heart, he felt a bond that was not there before.

For the last couple of years, he had spent his time making himself useful by teaching the young people in his tribe. It did not seem to matter that now he had tried to instruct a youth of another tribe. Maybe, he thought, it was the Spirits who brought about this chance meeting so that he could share his wisdom once more.

CHAPTER 9 - A SILENT RETREAT

His plan now was to slip silently off, if he headed back to the main path that ran around the southern part of the mountain, Little Bear would not be able to track him. To spend the last part of his life in this comfortable shelter was appealing, knowing what sort of end was coming. Quietly he arose and obscured the signs of his being there. He could not hide his tracks so easily out on the mountain side, but he laughed to himself as he envisioned Little Bear upon awaking and not immediately seeing him or the sign of his sitting there the night before. With his small satchel in hand, he looked back from just outside the recess to see Little Bear still sleeping. Broken Horn smiled and set off on his planned trail.

The morning was just about to break, the sky was clearing and the birds and animals were alive with their chatter after a stormy night. Long Cloud had arisen earlier, eaten a quick meal, had hid his camp and was heading back to the place he was the day before. As he first crested a small rise that was the rim on the far side of the lake and looked up to make sure Little Bear was not out where he could see him, a little sign could be seen of the fire within which was a good thing to see. He then scanned the hillside before moving into a position to wait for Little Bear. As he followed the trail above from north to south, to his horror he saw Broken Horn in the distance just going around the mountainside. Looking intently for any other movement; he saw none. He then looked back to the recess. There was no movement there, only the sign of a fire within. Fear now seized him. He had to know what had happened and if Little Bear was alright. Not losing control of himself, Long Cloud backed out, hurriedly circled back to the north side, which was the closest way, and sped around as noiselessly as he could. He considered the possibilities as he went along. If Little Bear was dead, he would track down and kill those responsible; if he was injured, he would have to tend him quickly and then track down those responsible and deal with them so that he could get Little Bear safely back to camp. If Little Bear was uninjured, he had to keep his presence secret so that Little Bear could finish his rite while he tracked down the person he had seen. He needed to gauge what danger Little Bear was in.

It took time to circle around with stealth to where he finally arrived at a point where he could peer in. The morning light lit up the inside of the recess even with the deer hide partially holding it out, and Long Cloud could see Little Bear with his buffalo skin pulled tightly around him inside the recess. All looked in order with no sign of a struggle. Straining his eyes Long Cloud could discern a slight movement as Little Bear stirred in his sleep. Though not completely sure, it did not seem he was injured. Long Cloud made the decision, though he wanted to stay and make absolutely sure that Little Bear was okay, to track down the one he had seen, find out what he was doing there, and then determine what to do next.

Broken Horn had a good head start, but he was older and slower, in less of a hurry. Both were trying to minimize their tracks knowing that Little Bear would otherwise notice the sign of their passing. With the trail going downhill, Broken Horn did not tire so it wasn't until he neared the main east west path that Long Cloud caught up with him. Seeing Broken Horn, a short distance ahead, he pulled out his knife, made a mad sprint forward leaping past him and stopping in his path.

Broken Horn stopped; his hand quickly held his knife out with the reflexes of a hardened warrior and took a defensive stance. He had forgotten that he had seen Long Cloud the day before and was caught unaware thinking only of the possibility of Little Bear coming up behind him. Now before him was a brave in his prime, Little Bear's protector, a guardian who was tasked to keep watch on Little Bear would mean a warrior of skill and endurance.

Long Cloud stared down on him, the one who had come between him and his charge. Though Little Bear did not look hurt, this he was not sure of. There was anger, anger that he had let someone get past him who was a possible threat to his nephew, his brother's son, the one whom he cared for like his own son. Not sure what to say or do that moment, he stood ready, regaining his breath and weighing up Broken Horn.

Broken Horn saw the danger and the trained warrior within him was in control, ready to strike, but wisdom prevailed preventing a needless fight. He wasn't sure what Long Cloud knew but felt it was best to clear up any misconception.

"I did not touch the youth," he said calmly, trying to keep all tension out of his voice, "Little Bear was unharmed and asleep when I left him."

He could see a slight look of relief pass over Long Cloud's face and stance, control of the moment he thought, I must keep it. Thinking it best to show no sign of aggression he relaxed a little, easing the grip on his knife and lowering it a little in hope Long Cloud would do so likewise.

"What were you doing with him," Long Cloud uttered with tautness in his voice that showed they were on a delicate edge. "Who are you and why were you there?"

"I am Broken Horn of the Yarric," he said proudly. He stood up a little straighter. He noted something in Long Cloud's face, as though he was unsure of his next step.

Long Cloud heard these words and was relieved at the thought of Little Bear not being hurt. He did not want to take a life needlessly and the anger was slowly starting to subside with the thought that Little Bear was safely sleeping in his camp. When Broken Horn mentioned his name there was something in the back of Long Cloud's mind, some memory, something that

106

wanted to get out, but he could not think of what it was.

Broken Horn sensed it as an ease in the tension. Long Cloud no longer seemed to be a danger. As Little Bear's guardian and now, he had no fear for his safety, the safety of the youth they both wanted to help was established. This interaction was a mistake, a misunderstanding that did not need to be. Perhaps, he thought, I can end it by fully answering his question. To give full effect to his words, Broken Horn lowered his knife, released all the tension and energy in his arms and shoulders, and in a low, weak voice spoke.

"I am Broken Horn of the Yarric, the owl has called my name and now I am but an old goat out in the wilderness."

Long Cloud stiffened up, old memories flooded in, old emotions rolled over him like a heard of buffalo. He looked at a deflated figure and knew that he must act. Quickly he changed his stance to one of readiness and tossed his knife from hand to hand. Broken Horn was startled as this was not what he had expected and with the reflexes of a warrior was ready to defend himself. Before him was a warrior ready to strike, one in his prime and Broken Horn was not confident that he could overcome him.

As soon as Broken Horn was set in his stance, Long Cloud tossed his knife to his left hand and made a slight lunge forward, Broken Horn quickly struck out and cut into Long Cloud's left forearm drawing a line of blood. Broken Horn smiled, the proud warrior was coming back and new confidence arose as his knife tasted blood.

"I am Broken Horn of the Yarric," he roared. "Warrior of many battles, I will not fall easily like an old goat in the wild!"

Long Cloud looked at the blood on Broken Horn's knife, saw this old man who had come to life again for one last battle, now was the time to strike. With the slightest of effort, he flipped his knife slightly forward, his right hand shooting out, catching the hilt and pushing it on towards Broken Horn's chest.

Broken Horn saw the movement, the speed and knew he was no match for it. Instinctively he tried to slash the arm away with his knife but knew he could not match the speed of Long Cloud; he knew that at that instant his death was at hand. He felt stunned as the blade caught him in the chest up to the hilt and pull out. He fell to his knees, his eyes dropped to see his knife still in his hand with Long Cloud's blood upon it. Broken Horn smiled, and fell over as death drew him in.

"Farewell Broken Horn of the Yarric, may you find honor among your forefathers as you go to them with the blood of your enemy on your blade."

Looking back to his arm to see what was needed, he picked up Broken Horn's satchel, cut a piece of leather from a short blanket within it and tied it around his forearm. He had left his supplies behind so Broken Horn's would have to do for the present. He drank some water and took a few bites of the food that was left in his satchel while he cleaned his knife and put it back in his sheaf. What to do now he thought. Something had to be done with Broken Horn's body. If left here in the open Little Bear would run across it on his way back and that might bring up question that the council would not want to answer. Also, buzzards would soon be flying about and that might bring some of Broken Horn's tribe around which would make it dangerous for Little Bear. Long Cloud looked over at Broken Horn's body.

"I do not know what you said or did while with Little Bear, maybe the Spirits had planned on your meeting him. Truly our paths were meant to cross. You did your part and I will not dishonor you.

Long Cloud took Broken Horn's knife from the hand that still clutched it and put it in his sheath, swung his satchel on his back, then lifted Broken Horn over his shoulder and set off, turning east when he came to the main path. He knew about where the Yarric had their camp, and if he could lay Broken Horn's body halfway between the path to his own camp and theirs, his body would be found and hopefully Little Bear would be safe as the Yarric would not look so far for the one who killed Broken Horn.

It was a long and hard morning, listening for the slightest

sound of anyone's approach. Two times he hurried into the brush when he thought he heard someone, but each was a false alarm. The sun was rising high and he knew he had to stop soon, if not due to being near the Yarric, just due to exhaustion from carrying Broken Horn so far. His body was covered in sweat as he labored in each step now. Though in good shape, he had walked a fair distance and it was taking a toll on his body and his reserves. Coming around a slight bend in the road he came face to face with four Yarric braves.

Long Cloud stopped as Chief Two Feathers and three young braves pulled up half a bow shot in front of him. One of the young braves instantly nocked an arrow and readied to shoot. Slowly Long Cloud laid Broken Horn down and then laid his satchel beside him. Chief Two Feathers walked firmly up to Long Cloud, looked down at his friend lying dead at their feet and back to Long Cloud.

"What is this," he said in a low firm voice that had anger barely in control in it.

Long Cloud stood there, breathing deeply from the effort of carrying Broken Horn such a long distance. His body was covered with sweat, Broken Horn's blood was on his right shoulder and back, and a little blood had seeped out from the leather strap on his left forearm. Long Cloud stood there, looking into Chief Two Feathers' eyes but not speaking even though he understood their tongue. The three other braves came up beside them, looked at Broken horn and glared at Long Cloud, one held his bow ready to let an arrow fly into Long Clouds' chest, the other two had pulled their knives and were ready to attack.

Long Cloud could see them but never let his eyes move from Chief Two Feathers. He knew he was outnumbered, too close for the arrow to miss its mark. He could handle the three braves if the bow was lowered but the Chief would be a challenge on his own if fighting all four. Besides, he was tired from carrying Broken Horn so long and needed rest, whatever happened, he needed some space to get his strength back.

Chief Two Feathers spoke again, this time in Long Clouds tongue, but his anger was more in check as he spoke.

"Why are you carrying Broken Horn?"

Long Cloud said nothing and this made the other brave angry and Running Water spoke up.

"I will shoot him where he stands, let me avenge Broken Horn's death."

The other braves quickly followed with their request to be the one to avenge Broken Horn.

"Hold!" shouted Chief Two Feathers. "If Broken Horn is to be avenged, I will be the one who gives out vengeance to the one who killed him!"

The three braves quickly became silent not wanting to face Chief Two Feathers' anger.

Long Cloud felt a little relieved, a glimmer of hope as Running Water lowered his bow and the other two braves lowered their knives. Chief Two Feathers had complete control and no one dare challenge him. Now Long Cloud waited to gain all the strength he could, if it came to a fight with Chief Two Feathers alone, he had a chance, once the Chief was defeated a quick attack on the surprised three braves was possible so Long Cloud just stood there looking at Chief Two Feathers and waited.

Chief Two Feathers was wise and did not like to act rashly, he was curious about this turn of events. Broken Horn was on his way to Spirit Mountain to most likely die a slow death, now here he was, dead with a knife wound to his heart and carried by an unknown brave who would not answer him. He looked Long Cloud up and down, he was of the Kengeia tribe which was to the south, what was he doing here?

"You are Kengeia, they do not know your tongue," he motioned to his braves with a slight nod of his head, "but I do, why do you not talk?"

Long Cloud just looked at him, no malice or anger, no emotion at all.

A bird fluttered in the trees just behind Long Cloud and to his left, Chief Two Feathers glanced quickly and noticed the slightest flinch in Long Cloud as he did. He looked back in the direction of the bird and saw Spirit Mountain was in the distance. Yes, something was at Spirit Mountain that made Long Cloud nervous, that he wanted to remain hidden. This puzzle was a challenge to figure out and Chief Two Feathers was not one to shy away from a challenge. Broken Horn was going to Spirit Mountain, what had he seen or done and was that why Broken Horn was killed? Chief Two Feathers thought, the Kengeia are not warriors out to fight, they follow the buffalo and trade a bit, so the answer had to do with Spirit Mountain which was out of their range, a quest or rite he mused.

Chief Two Feathers looked at Long Cloud closely noticing the sweat and blood, no weapon but a knife. He then saw that a little blood had flowed from a wound on his left forearm from under a leather strap. Going over to Broken Horn, Chief Two Feathers saw his knife still in his sheaf which was strange if this was a battle between enemies, why was the knife returned to its sheaf? Bending down he slowly pulled the knife out, it had blood on it. He held it up for the others braves to see.

"Broken Horn seems to have the blood of his enemy, the blood of combat on his knife. Our fathers will welcome him with honor!" He said this loud and with pride. This brought smiles to the three brave who were standing there, to know Broken Horn had died with honor brought a change in their mood.

Putting the knife carefully back, Chief Two Feathers stood back up and looked at Long Cloud, his knife was worn like he was right-handed but the wound was like that of one who fought left-handed. This puzzled Chief Two Feathers; there were many puzzling matters here.

He reached into a pouch behind him and pulled out a piece of deer jerky and tossed it to Long Cloud aiming for the center of his chest. With lightning speed his right hand reached out with a sense of grace and grabbed it while never moving his eyes from Chief Two Feathers' eyes.

Chief Two Feathers knew of a few of the Kengeia but had heard of one who was a great hunter and who fought bravely in battle, a brave of honor who had a reputation that was known by many tribes.

"Long Cloud," the Chief said, "Long Cloud of the Kengeia."

Long Cloud stiffened a bit, he had been found out and that meant there could be retaliation on his tribe. But what could he do, he would not lie, for honor's sake as well as it was dangerous to be caught up in an untruth, so he held his tongue.

"You are a puzzle Long Cloud, you killed Broken Horn but I cannot see why? You let him draw blood, Broken Horn would not have attacked you in surprise so you must have let him cut you, he could not have moved fast enough unless you let him."

Chief Two Feathers' brow wrinkled as he thought about the possibilities, he had the time to think and making right decisions was important, especially when they dealt with the relations of other tribes. Looking back to Spirit Mountain, Chief Two Feathers considered what he knew, Broken Horn's call, Long Cloud killed Broken Horn, Long Cloud let him draw first blood, an honorable Long Cloud who hesitated about something on Spirit Mountain, yet he risked a lot to bring Broken Horn's body back where he might be caught and killed. Truly the Spirits were involved in these events but what was their purpose? Then an idea came to him.

Without turning from Long Cloud, Chief Two Feathers spoke out in a voice of command to his braves.

"Take Broken Horn back to camp and prepare all for the burial of a warrior, a warrior fallen in battle with the blood of his enemy upon his knife. I will take care of this brave."

There was no arguing with Chief Two Feathers even though they wished to stay they knew better than to question or delay in following his commands. They quickly picked up Broken Horn and headed back to their camp with a few glances over their shoulders.

Long Cloud was not sure what was going to happen next, but if he was to have to fight Chief Two Feathers and not have to contend with the other braves at the same time, he had a good chance of staying alive. Every moment that went by was a little more time for strength to returned to him, so he did not move, but just stood there trying to be ready for whatever was to come.

After enough time had passed that Chief Two Feathers knew his braves were out of sight and well on their way, he spoke in a more relaxed tone.

"Long Cloud, it would be an honor to face you in battle," he paused a moment.

Long Cloud was sizing him up, the Yarric had different beliefs and were quicker to go into battle, but they also believed in honor which he could respect.

"Broken Horn was a mighty warrior and my friend," he paused again and it seemed that his eyes were now turned within, seeing times of the past. "It saddened me when the owl called his name, knowing the kind of death that awaited him. Tonight, there will be a big celebration to honor him, having died as a warrior and not as an old dog alone in the woods."

"I shall not forget this, the gift that you have given to Broken Horn and our tribe."

Again, he paused, watching Long Cloud, giving him an opportunity to speak. Long Cloud said nothing which was his way, but now he was able to relax though he showed it not. Looking back to Spirit Mountain, Chief Two Feathers continued.

"The one who is still on Spirit Mountain, the rite or quest being done must be finished soon. My braves will be busy for the next couple days, but then without my bidding they will attempt to track you down. If you leave a light trail in less than half a day's travel this path comes to a rocky trail that continues on westward. That would be the best place for them to lose track of you and you can easily circle back to Spirit Mountain."

Still looking at Long Cloud, to have heard of this braves reputation of honor and then to see it in action brought out a warm feeling of respect. He wished that Long Cloud would speak to him, thought there was not much to say and with unfinished business on Spirit Mountain maybe it was best left unsaid. Knowing of Long Cloud's journey and seeing that he now had no supplies with him Chief Two Feathers unfastened his water skin and tossed it to Long Cloud.

"I would be honored to have one such as you to be called friend, Long Cloud, go in peace."

With that Chief Two Feathers turned and headed back to his camp. Long Cloud watched him until the trail turned from view and then he turned around and started at a quick trot down the trail on the long trip back to Spirit Mountain.

In a little distance Long Cloud came to a small stream that crossed the path. He stopped for a rest, to clean the blood off him and ate the small piece of jerky that he was still carrying in his hand. He thought of the events that had occurred that day, so much had happened in such a short amount of time, more than what one could have imaged to take place. Truly the Spirits were at work. There were many questions to be answered, the most important of which had to do with Broken Horn and Little Bear. It would be several days before Little Bear spoke of his quest before the council and only then would there be answers. But a question that would not be answered was, was Broken Horn meeting Little Bear by chance or was it by design of the Spirits? Whatever the answer, to make it back to Little Bear's camp by night fall he must press ahead, and so off Long Cloud bound down the trail to lead some astray and then to get back to his watch.

CHAPTER 10 - BACK TO THE QUEST

Little Bear awoke to a dying fire and the light of morning streaming into his shelter. His first thoughts were to the dreams of that night, visions that his mind was mulling over sparked on by the exchange with Broken Horn. Suddenly remembering Broken Horn, he jumped up and looked around, all was in its place but there was no sign of Broken Horn at hand. Looking to where he had sat the night before it looked as if no one had been sitting there. But he had seen him eat a skewer of meat, it was no dream. Quickly going to the edge of the recess he scanned the hillside but saw nothing but a few insects buzzing about.

Little Bear did not think to search for tracks leading away. Even a seasoned warrior could not pass on that wet mountain side without leaving a trace of his passing, but Little Bear was drawn back to where Broken Horn had been sitting, and there was no sign there. How does one track a spirit if they leave no impression? Broken Horn had come and gone unnoticed; surely, he was a spirit Little Bear concluded. A shiver ran down Little Bear's back, he had been in the presence of a spirit, a thing only told of in tales by the fireside and now he had lived through such a night.

Little Bear put some more wood on the fire, there was comfort in a fire when one was all alone, and he sat near it for its warmth as he thought. The memories of the previous night were fresh and he went over and over all that was said and seen. Little Bear revisited his vision and repeating Broken Horn's words to make sure he did not forget anything. His concentration was broken as his stomach started to growl.

"The words of the Spirits are a rare thing but the stomach waits for no man." Little Bear said this softly with a laugh as he looked down to his belly The fresh meat was gone but there was plenty of dried. Pulling out a few pieces, he slowly chewed away while looking at the spot where Broken Horn had sat the night before trying to remember what he looked like and how his voice sounded.

After a while Little Bear got up and looked out over the lake.

"It is time I go," he said softly, "time for me to go back home."

Remembering his own vow and the words of Broken Horn, Little Bear ventured out and brought in several arm loads of fresh wood for the next person to us in this little recess. After neatly stacking the wood, oldest in front, new in back, he stopped for one last meal. When this was done, he went down to fill his water skin and drink deeply one last time. Going through the recess, gathering his possessions and then looking out over the little lake he felt sadness in leaving. It was a comfortable camp and a sense of peace could be felt in the air, a good place to listen for a vision, a good place to learn to listen.

The sun was rising, and there was a long road ahead. Little Bear thought of his tribe and all the activity that would be going on, he thought of his mom's cooking and remembered that all he had was dried deer meat until he returned home. A vision of White Fawn came to mind, remembering how she looked before he had left and a warm feeling of desire came to him. In a flash he was off, thinking of good food and friends while he stepped over signs of Broken Horn's passing without noticing.

The trip home looked as if it were going to be quiet and uneventful as he had enough dried meat to last without need to hunt. He was cautious as he neared the east west path, listening and watching for movement and thereby missing the slight sign of a struggle that Long Cloud had tried to cover earlier that day.

He ran with contentment in his heart that his rite would soon be over with the conclusion being that he was now a man, a brave of his tribe. The combination of the fear that he had felt that he was ready and the words of Broken Horn that he was no one special or greater than others of his tribe, brought him to a place where he accepted who he was, just a new brave of the Kengeia and nothing more. There was comfort in this, no false image that he had to live up to. Somewhere in the future his courage would be tested, the Spirits would speak and he would listen, but now all he had to do was be a brave of the tribe and grow in strength and wisdom which sounded so easy.

The sun had long gone over the mountain when Long Cloud came back in sight of the little lake from the west over the shoulder of the mountain. With his keen eyes, from a distance he saw no sign of a fire from where the recess lay. Cautiously moving closer, he soon saw that the deerskin that was stretched out over the mouth of the recess was no longer in its place. Going to the trail leading back to the south he saw Little Bear's tracks heading back to the tribe, a welcome sign knowing they would be back to the safety of the tribe before any Yarric would come looking for them. It would be dark soon and Long Cloud was tired and knew better than to travel on an old trail on a mountainside at night. Going to where he had stored his supplies, he gathered his possessions and returned to the recess. A secure place to spend the night and a large store of dry wood, he would get a good rest and be off in the morning. Unless Little Bear pressed hard Long Cloud felt he would catch up to him within two days, not what he had planned but it was what it was.

The next day Long Cloud was careful until he was long past the east west path and felt there was little chance of running into any of the Yarric. He pressed hard in a strong lope taking little time to rest even though all he saw was sign of Little Bear's passing. It was not until half a day from the tribe that Little Bear could occasionally be seen in the distance which allowed Long Cloud to slow down his pace.

The plan with Rolling Thunder was for him to circle around to the east side of camp and leave a sign on a low plateau where two boulders stood on the very edge of a steep drop. Rolling Thunder was to leave a piece of wood on the right boulder as a sign to come to camp right away, a rock for him to come in one day, and nothing meant all was well and to come in from the south in two days ensuring all saw his coming. Likewise, Long Cloud would leave a piece of wood on the left boulder if he had important news and needed Rolling Thunder to meet him behind the boulders, a rock meaning he needed to come in one day, and nothing if all was well and he would follow their plans. No one was to know that Long Cloud had been following Little Bear and so the presence of Long Cloud being down in the south was necessary to keep anyone from drawing conclusions about his helping Little Bear. Long Cloud had no problem in evading eyes as he made his way to the plateau and with little need for thought, left a piece of wood on the left boulder and waited.

Little Bear came trotting into camp beaming with joy as his friends gathered around. To his surprise White Fawn came up to him with tears in her eyes and gave him a hug and then stepped back. That warm feeling again flooded in and he had a desire to hold her close, White Fawn had snared his heart before one of her friends had a chance. He was now considered a man unlike most of his friends but these were still his friends and he was glad to see them again. Soon it would be time to join the men but that could wait as now it was the time for friends to come together and celebrate, but with special eyes towards White Fawn. Word spread quickly and Red Bird came running to see her son, her only son. So many nights of worry were shed off in a moment, like the pains of birth forgotten when she beheld her son for the first time; and like the time he was born, she had to hold him even if all of his friends were around watching. Cries of happiness and of excitement abounded as more of the tribe came up and gathered around Little Bear and Red Bird.

Word came to Black Eagle and Rolling Thunder and they smiled on hearing that Little Bear's quest was complete. A message was sent to Little Bear to get something to eat, clean up, and then come to Black Eagle's tepee. This was a big event for the tribe, but even bigger for Little Bear, and Black Eagle did not want to take from him and his friends too much of this time of celebration. Black Eagle sat outside his tepee to await Little Bear while Rolling Thunder left silently to see what message there was from Long Cloud.

As most of the tribe was gathering around Little Bear it was easy for Rolling Thunder to move quietly and unnoticed out of camp and to the nearby plateau. An easy walk and he hoped and expected to see nothing on the left boulder as all the cheerful noise in camp seemed to relate that there was no problem that required a change in plans. Looking from a distance he paused, a piece of wood laid upon the left boulder could easily be seen, Rolling Thunder's heart felt heavy at its sight and his head momentarily dropped from the change of expectations. This was not foreseen as Little Bear's arrival was being met by a festive atmosphere and he had not come directly to Black Eagle or himself to tell of any troubles. The answer would soon enough be revealed and Rolling Thunder, after making sure no one was watching, made his way up to the two boulders to meet Long Cloud.

Long Cloud was waiting on the back side of the boulders, resting in a comfortable spot, being warmed by the sun's rays as it was slowly sinking in the west. He had seen Rolling Thunder coming earlier so he did not stir as he heard the sound of someone climbing the plateau. A smile appeared upon his face as Rolling Thunder rounded the stones and sat beside him. It was good to be back with his friend, his tribe, even though his task was not yet complete.

"It is good to see you back, Long Cloud, we have been wondering how your task was going," Rolling Thunder said with a little relief in his voice, seeing that Long Cloud was in good condition and looked relaxed. "When Little Bear came back into camp all seemed well so I was surprised to see your need to talk."

Long Cloud quickly related how Broken Horn spent some time with Little Bear, his own interaction with Broken Horn,

Chief Two Feathers and his braves, and his warning that in two or three days there would probably be a couple of braves out tracking him.

"I led a false trail to an area of rock and circled back from there," Long Cloud continued, "if it is those three young braves then most likely they will lose my trail. Still, I thought it might be wise to have someone watch the path from Spirit Mountain to give warning if anyone comes from there."

Rolling Thunder nodded in agreement. "I do not expect that they would be able to track you my friend, but then it is an easy thing to do to have a few on guard and it is best to be prepared."

Leaning back and looking to the sky as he thought for a moment, Rolling Thunder continued. "Running Bear and Gray Dawn are young and would feel honored to stand guard. I will tell them they are to ensure no one has followed Little Bear and that should be enough." Rolling Thunder smiled and gave a little laugh. "My son Running Bear has been pressing to have his rite ever since Little Bear left. I wish it was because he was ready and not envy that drives him. This task should help quiet him down a bit and maybe help him to get closer to the day he is ready for his rite."

Long Cloud smiled. "We too were impatient for our day to come and it must have been very tiring for our fathers to endure; is this not the way it is with all boys?" And they both laughed.

Looking at his friend he noticed his satchel looked pretty empty, Rolling Thunder frowned.

"You have done well Long Cloud; Little Bear is safely back as are you. I will not send you off in want after all that you have done, stay here and I will come back with fresh supplies to last you until your return."

Looking to the south and seeing the plains that opened up under clear blue skies, Rolling Thunder concluded, "Come in from the south at midday in two days' time. We will meet with the council to hear what you saw then. On that evening we will bring Little Bear in to relate his experiences and interpret what the Spirits had to say. It will be best that we continue as planned and no one knows you were there. Speak of Broken Horn only to the council."

With that said, Rolling Thunder got up, and peered around the rock to ensure no one was in sight.

"I will leave the supplies below," he said with a warm smile looking back at Long Cloud, "I will look forward to your return and will consider your words carefully."

Rolling Thunder then stepped out of view to descend to the floor below and make his way back to camp. Long Cloud got up and removed the wood that he had placed on the boulder so not to draw attention to the spot and sat down in the warm sun again. He had kept up a fast pace the last couple of days and was in need of rest. Having given a brief account to Rolling Thunder and now that Little Bear was safely back in the tribe was a relief of such a weight of responsibility that he was surprised by its absence. Long Cloud had been responsible for many things in the past, been near death on numerous occasions, but this time was different. He was keeping watch on Little Bear, his brother's son, Red Bird's only child, and as he now realized, he looked at Little Bear as his own son. With little chance of anyone coming that way and his being hidden from view, Long Cloud leaned back, feeling the warmth of the sun on his now relaxed frame and was soon enjoying some much-needed sleep.

The sun was sitting lower as Long Cloud opened his eyes and he wondered how he could have slept so long. Slowly rising, stretching, and then shaking the stiffness from his limbs he looked around. He ensured his solitude, then looking between the two boulders and down below, he saw a satchel. Again, looking around and seeing no one, he made his way down and retrieved the bundle, a well-stocked supply along with a neatly rolled up deerskin that was gladly received.

Two days later Long Cloud came walking into camp with a freshly shot deer draped across his shoulder. He drew little attention as he often came and went without much notice, and since a couple of days had passed since Little Bear's return the two events were not connected. He walked through camp and up to Red Bird's tepee and stopped. He could hear her within and his heart felt faint. He wondered how he could feel such fear in facing her when he did not flinch when face to face with Chief Two Feathers and his braves.

"Red Bird," he called softly, and stood there waiting.

Red Bird stepped out quickly, curtly he thought. She stood there sternly looking up at him.

"Well, the mighty Long Cloud has returned, bearing a deer for me I suppose?"

Her voice was sharp and cut deeply like a quick stab of a knife to the heart. He felt a burning sensation in his face as he blushed at her hard stare.

"While you were gone another brave has come into my tepee," she said with a sly grin.

Long Cloud faltered, caught himself under the weight of the deer and stood still as he crumbled on the inside. He was being rejected, he thought, because he was not there during the time Little Bear was on his rite, when she needed comfort and support. Who could have taken advantage of his being off, what other brave had come between him and Red Bird he wondered, hurt turning to anger. He could not tell her the truth about where he was and how he had to be near Little Bear. No excuse could be offered so he just stood there.

Red Bird saw his pain which confirmed what she had known for a long time; she had captured his heart completely. But pain was not what she meant to impart; she broke into a huge smile, pushed the deer from his shoulder and as it dropped, she hugged him tight.

"Little Bear, my Little Bear is now a brave, a man of the tribe," and she half laughed and half cried and squeezed Long Cloud tighter.

Long Cloud was totally disarmed, he had worried about this meeting, afraid of what she might say, and then crushed by her first words, now he could barely stand as he was held in her arms. He pulled his arm free that she had pinned to his side and hugged her tight, feeling a restoring of his soul as they hugged each other. He lowered his head and rested it on her brow, and Red Bird felt the tears flow down from above and she knew one day she would be his.

The first council meeting went quickly. Long Cloud was matter of fact with what he saw and only after he had related the events did he venture the opinion that it was in the Spirits' plans for Broken Horn to make his appearance. "We must listen carefully to what Little Bear says for us to know the truth in these matters. I do not know what was said between Little Bear and Broken Horn. This was not how we expected the rite to go, but one never knows what to expect from the wisdom of the Spirits."

Black Eagle then reiterated that Little Bear was not to know of Long Cloud's presence, to ask whatever questions they needed, but discussion about the events would be held after Little Bear left. The second council meeting came, this one with Little Bear after the evening meal. All the council members sat around the fire in Black Eagle's tepee as Rolling Thunder led Little Bear in and sat him down in a space between himself and Black Eagle. The council sat and listened as Little Bear told of his quest beginning when he first left until his return. Many were the questions about his vision and many about Broken Horn and what he thought. The evening was well advanced when all questions were finished and Black Eagle ended the session.

"You did well in remembering your quest Little Bear; you did well indeed. There is much to think about and we will be here long into the night, but there is no need for you to stay."

Little Bear looked disappointed about not staying and listening to what the council thought but Black Eagle gave him no choice.

"Go out and enjoy your friends tonight. We will talk again tomorrow and discuss our understanding." Black Eagle stood and led Little Bear out. "We will call you tomorrow after the evening meal and will discuss your visions then."

A firm hand on his back with a little pressure and the pleasant but set look in his eye told Little Bear to be off without a question. The council took this time to stretch but remained quiet until Little Bear was out of sight and the sound of his retreat faded away. The Spirits' direction for Little Bear, to be a warrior, hunter, and messenger of the Spirits, as well as his rite was unusual from the start. To travel so far and for the length of days was even more unusual. The council was in a sense of wonderment from the beginning, but now they were speechless at the completion of Little Bear's rite. Looking from person to person, they did not know where to even start with their questions, much less with their understanding.

Slowly the council sat back down around the fire, perplexed at that series of happenings that was far from what they had expected. Helpful though it was to have heard Long Cloud's account before listening to Little Bear, to understand the events was a challenge that they were not ready for. Black Eagle was last to sit. It was quiet except for the crackling of the fire before them. No one knew where to start and after looking back and forth all eyes settled on Black Eagle looking for some kind of guidance. Black Eagle knew he must take the lead, he being the medicine man ought best be able to decipher the meaning, but this was a difficult set of events to understand.

To gain a bit of time to think, Black Eagle pulled out his pipe and slowly filled it with tobacco. Taking the time for the common task of packing his pipe, slowly puffing away with a hot coal from the fire to light it, and then passing the pipe down the line of the council members gave him time to let Little Bear's words sink in and to consider their meaning. Looking into the fire, he knew he had to begin. "My friends," he stated in a tone not of evasion but as a matter-of-fact comment, "this will take much wisdom to fully understand what has happened and what the Spirits have said and done. I welcome your words of wisdom in this."

Many heads nodded in agreement and a few added low words of accent. The honesty of Black Eagle put them at ease and they all wanted to offer what help they could. It was going to be a long night in which they all would take part.

"Long Cloud, you have done well in watching over Little Bear and the knowledge which we have gained through your eyes is invaluable in our understanding this matter. To know that Broken Horn was a brave of the Yarric and not a spirit tells us quite a lot. To know that the owl had called his name tells us the Spirits had meant for him and Little Bear to meet and it was meant for you and Broken Horn's path to cross. I would ask you, Long Cloud, now that you have heard what Little Bear had to say, what do you make of what has happened?"

Long Cloud by nature was short in words, usually expressing what needed to be said in as few as needed, but what needed to be said he did not know and this was unusual for him. Best, he thought, to share his thinking and let others add their insight.

"I saw in Little Bear the beginnings of a brave, not only in body but in mind," he stated, looking towards Black Eagle but seeing the events of the last few days in his mind. "His physical strength and knowledge are there, of this I am sure. I watched him think and consider his actions on several occasions and he chose according to honor and not ease; I am proud of him."

At this the council members nodded and murmured words of approval. To hear that a new brave was more than an overgrown boy that only sought his own comfort, ease, or passions to be pleased was welcomed. This had been a concern for several of the council members, since Little Bear was on the young side to partake in his rite. These words quelled those concerns.

"I saw," Long Cloud continued, "him make several choices. I saw him falter but for a moment and then rise to the honor of the tribe. What happened in that recess on the side of Spirit Mountain I cannot say but from what I did see, there is no question that Little Bear was meant to believe that Broken Horn was a Spirit. Whether it was the Spirits' or Broken Horn's idea to leave no sign of his being there within the recess I do not know, but I am sure, it was the Spirits who wanted Little Bear to think that he was a Spirit. Also, I would say after listening to Chief Two Feathers, Broken Horn was a brave of honor. I believe he had no ill will in misleading Little Bear and that this was also the will of the Spirits."

At that, Long Cloud was silent; he turned his gaze towards the fire even though he saw nothing but his own thoughts. Black Eagle knew this was all that Long Cloud was going to say for now and was quite appreciative for it. With a look to the rest of the council that implied openness for opinion, questions, and discussion, the meeting went on for a long time and many logs were burned that night. Morning was not far off when Black Eagle was ready to speak his final pronouncement.

"I thank you my friends as you have helped me sort out a series of actions that have never before been heard of. If the Spirits have acted in such a way in the past, I do not know of it and it is best that the truth of this tale stays here so that Little Bear never knows who Broken Horn was; this is what the Spirits would have wanted. Some would think that Broken Horn just happened on Little Bear's rite. I do not believe that was the case. Broken Horn was intricately tied to Little Bear and Long Cloud. All this was planned long before their meeting had taken place."

A murmur of astonishment was heard around the fire as the council looked back and forth from one another and then to Black Eagle.

"The Spirits guide not only us but also all the other tribes as well; who are we to think that we are so special that the Spirits single us out? No, their plans go far beyond our tribe only."

Again, there was a murmur of astonishment; astonishment by some that the Spirits would consider it worthy to deal equally with tribes like the Yarric.

"Long Cloud was the fulfillment of Broken Horn's life; Broken Horn was the start of Little Bear's life as a brave of the Kengeia."

Once again there was an astonished murmuring around the fire at the thought of these two tribes being linked together.

"I believed Broken Horn read Little Bear's vision rightly. The Spirits have great plans for Little Bear and he must learn to hear when the Spirits speak, learn to see visions and understand what they say, and then to act as they direct. We are all to give our aid in teaching Little Bear what we know as this is the will of the Spirits."

There was quiet as the council looked back and forth to each other then slowly their thoughts came into line with Black Eagle's thinking as they could see how all the events and Little Bear's vision came together to be of the plans of the Spirits. What was to come in their future must be of great importance for the Spirits to express their message in such a forceful way. Turbulent times were ahead but now the tribe would have time to prepare. As the council began to grasp these thoughts, they looked to Black Eagle and spoke in agreement to his reading of the recent events. The dawn was near and it was time for a final word to all.

"My friends," Black Eagle started, "it is important that Little Bear does not know the truth about Broken Horn, remember that. I will give a reading of Little Bear's quest to him tonight as we all gather to give him our support and welcome him as a brave of our tribe. Listen to this and let it be a guide as you impart what knowledge you have for him."

"It is now morning, go and rest for our work has just begun."

It was not until the day was half gone that Little Bear saw any of the council and the first was Long Cloud that he saw approaching him.

"You must be curious Little Bear about the thoughts of the council." Long Cloud said in a surprisingly warm way. This was the first time he had the opportunity to speak to Little Bear since the beginning of his quest and he was both proud of him and relieved at seeing him safely back within the tribe.

Curious, Little Bear thought, does not even come close to how I feel, but he held his tongue on this matter.

"It is good to see you Long Cloud, and apparently mom was glad to see you too since you were off on some mission of Rolling Thunder's to the south." Little Bear had a smile on his face knowing he was making Long Cloud uneasy. The feelings between Long Cloud and Red Bird were well known; the only question was when they would admit it to each other. Though not quick in word, Long Cloud lost no time in changing the subject back to Little Bear.

"Tonight, at the central fire Rolling Thunder will call you forward and Black Eagle will give the interpretation of what the Spirits spoke through your vision."

With that said, Long Cloud quickly turned and left. Little Bear smiled with a little chuckle. Maybe, he mused, he could have gotten more out of Long Cloud had he not had a little fun at his expense. Now came the long hours which seemed even longer since he ruined any chance of getting clues out of Long Cloud but he took consolation in remembering Long Cloud's face at his remark.

CHAPTER 11 - THE COMPLETION OF THE RITE

Finally, the fire was lit, the evening meals eaten, and the tribe gathered around to see the final part of Little Bear's rite as Black Eagle would speak of the Spirits leading Little Bear as he came into manhood in the tribe. This was a big event for all as the tribe was truly a family and Little Bear considered a son or brother to all. The tribe sat and talked as the stars overhead came out on this clear spring night. The mood was more sedate as compared to the excitement at the start of the rite and as Little Bear's return had passed, now was the time for the speech by Black Eagle and the formal acceptance given by Rolling Thunder.

Red Bird had prepared a new set of buckskin leggings for Little Bear which he proudly wore. Red Bird's friends gathered around her remarking what a fine image he was of a new brave. "Soon," they giggled, "there will be new additions to the tribe!" It was now assumed that White Fawn would soon be Little Bear's wife as these women watched closely the interactions of the youth of the tribe. Red Bird was so happy to have brought a son up to manhood for the tribe and though only one, he was her legacy, her gift for the continuance of the family, the tribe.

The drums began to beat and the noise of the tribe quieted down. From out of Black Eagle's tepee came Rolling Thunder followed by the council and they walked slowly to their places at the head of the fire. As they sat, the drums beat on for a few moments until Black Eagle emerged wearing his ceremonial garb which was the signal for the drums to stop. Slowly walking to his place between Rolling Thunder and Long Cloud, chanting slowly as he went. He stayed standing upon arriving and continued chanting while looking to the sky as small embers floated up seemingly joining the stars. When he finally stopped chanting, a smile emerged upon his face, a smile that showed a warm pleasure in seeing the tribe before him. After scanning the faces, he focused his eyes on Little Bear.

"Little Bear," he called loud enough for all to hear, "come forward and receive the guidance of the Spirits."

Little Bear could not hold back his excitement and the grin on his face could not be contained no matter how hard he tried. Rising to a standing position he moved forward in a motion that felt more like he was floating, being blown by the wind in an inescapable movement that brought him between Black Eagle and the fire that blazed behind him. He swayed back and forth slightly no matter how hard he tried to stand still causing him to fear that he might fall over. The red light of the flames lit up and accented a smile on Black Eagle's weathered face that also could not be contained; a smile that came from a heart that was sharing the joy that radiated out from Little Bear. Looking quickly about the fire it could be seen that this smile was contagious and had infected the whole tribe with its pure and simple pleasure. Black Eagle stepped forward and put his hands on Little Bear's shoulders.

"Little Bear, the Spirits are pleased as we give heed to their signs and follow their lead."

Looking up over Little Bear's head he spoke out in a loud voice for all to hear.

"The Spirits are looking down on us tonight as we sit under the stars."

Heads turned up seeing the constellations that spanned the night sky, looking, hoping to see the Spirits looking back down upon them.

Black Eagle continued after a small pause. "Our fathers are up there seeing our tribe here below. They see us, their children and are glad that we still remember them and the ways that they passed on to us. We all know that they called upon Little Bear, called upon him to meet them at Spirit Mountain only a few days ago."

Eyes went from Little Bear to the direction that Spirit Mountain lay and back to Little Bear again. Most members of the tribe were still in awe that anyone on their rite would be sent so far into possible danger. Truly this was a mysterious sign in itself that they hoped to have explained before the night was over.

"There he was given a vision and the Spirits spoke to him."

A murmur went about the fire and Black Eagle waited until it subsided.

"Three messages were given, three things for Little Bear and for us to know. They have chosen Little Bear for a purpose, though not revealed now, the Spirits will use Little Bear in the future."

Again, there was a murmur with voices of astonishment as they wondered why the Spirits would have need of Little Bear and their tribe. When this quieted down Black Eagle began again.

"The Spirits have welcomed Little Bear into his new position as a brave of our tribe, young though he might be."

Little Bear felt self-conscious with everyone looking at him from behind and being called young, but he stood still, he was now being accepted as a man.

"And finally, the council was given charge to train Little Bear in the reading of signs, in listening for the Spirits, and in understanding as they give their knowledge, wisdom, and instruction."

Little Bear thought it was odd that Black Eagle did not speak more of his vision or of Broken Horn, but maybe he thought that part of the rite was just for him to know.

Black Eagle smiled as he looked into Little Bear's face, a warm smile not like that towards a child but towards a friend. Taking his hands from Little Bear's shoulder, Black Eagle turned, went back and sat at his place between Rolling Thunder and Long Cloud. Rolling Thunder immediately got up and came to Little Bear, grasping him so firmly with his powerful arms that he felt he was going to be crushed.

"Little Bear, is a brave of our tribe ," he spoke loud so that the tribe could hear. "He has acted with honor above all else. The way of children is for children, the way of the brave is a sacred honor that has been carried on from our fathers' fathers' fathers, and many of his fathers before him."

"Every person in the tribe is important and every task is one that must be done. Little Bear, the direction of the Spirits given for you is different. You will train as a hunter and help supply the needs of the tribe. You will train as a warrior to lead the tribe in times of battle if that time comes. You will train in reading the signs of the Spirits, to keep in their will and receive help as they so deem your need. And in all of this, you will act in honor as our fathers before us and our children will after us."

There was a pause and Little Bear sensed that Rolling Thunder was through speaking to him. This was not enough, there were questions that he still had about his vision and about Broken Horn that he wanted to have answered. The events that had happened on his rite had never been heard of before that he knew of and must therefore be of great importance. He needed answers. Rolling Thunder could feel Little Bear tense up under his hands that still held onto his shoulders and could guess what was going through Little Bear's mind. Speaking softly so that only Little Bear could hear, Rolling Thunder whispered.

"There is wisdom for you to learn, your vision yet to be explained by the council as each member imparts their knowledge to you. You are on a path with a future that has been foreseen by the Spirits. We will help you prepare for what is to come. In the coming days we will answer what questions we can, but not tonight."

Now speaking loudly for all to hear with a proud voice,

Rolling Thunder addressed Little Bear., "You are Little Bear, brave of the Kengeia, the continuation of our tribe!"

Rolling Thunder gave him a squeeze with his powerful hands and Little Bear knew that there would be no more answers tonight. He turned and faced the tribe who were all sitting about the fire watching. He saw smiles and excitement in their faces. They were happy for him; they were his family. No longer was Little Bear a boy, he was Little Bear the brave and it was his responsibility to care for them like every other brave of the tribe.

It was at this moment that everything looked different. Fully feeling accepted as a man of the tribe now that the rite was completed, he accepted this new role. Looking over the tribe his eyes came across White Fawn and he paused, a longing filled his heart and he knew soon was the time that she would share his tepee.

The drums started beating and Little Bear smiled, looked to the sky and gave a cry of delight. His friends echoed the call and soon there was dancing all about.

Rolling Thunder looked at Black Eagle, Long Cloud, and the rest of the council and smiled, all was well with the tribe.

CHARACTERS

Characters:

Little Bear – 15 year old main character

Black Eagle – Medicine man

Rolling Thunder – Chief

Three Suns – Little Bear's father

Red Bird – Little Bear's mother

Long Cloud – Little Bear's uncle

Running Bear – Rolling Thunder's son

Four Horns, Grey Eyes, Silver Fox, Running Wolf – Tribal elders

Morning Calf, Night Rider, Red Cloud – Medicine men

Kengeia – Little Bear's tribe

Yarric – Unfriendly tribe to the north with Spirit Mountain in its territory

Yarric members – Broken Horn, Running Water, Chief Two Feathers